ISLAND SECRETS

Darcy Rice

KISMET is a trademark of Meteor Publishing Corporation.

Copyright © 1991 Darcy Rice
Cover Art Copyright © 1991 Terry Widener

All rights reserved.

No part of this book may be reproduced or altered in any retrieval system, or transmitted, in any form, by any means (mechanical, electronic, photographic, photocopying, recording, or otherwise) without prior written permission of the publisher, Meteor Publishing Corporation, 3369 Progress Drive, Bensalem, PA 19020.

A KISMET™ Romance

METEOR PUBLISHING CORPORATION
Bensalem, Pennsylvania

For Rowley

DARCY RICE

Darcy Rice lives in San Clemente, California, and Kailua-Kona, Hawaii. Darcy loves reading, writing, and family times at the beach with one baby son and two unmanageable dogs.

Other KISMET books by Darcy Rice:

No. 25 *LOVE WITH INTEREST*

PROLOGUE

The hull of the boat cut a strong swath through the low, powerful swells, sending a fine mist spraying up on both sides with the sharp slap of each impact. The setting sun had disappeared behind the island's ridgeline a half hour earlier, and the last golden light of the afternoon was rapidly fading, giving way to the purple glow of dusk. The translucent blue waves became opaque, black peaks, like an endless range of distant mountains.

The man at the boat's wheel stood up to see more clearly in the diminishing light. Brisk, salty wind fingered carelessly through his thick blond hair. He pushed it out of his eyes with a rough gesture. Narrowing his eyes to intense blue slits, he checked his heading against the dimly lighted compass, then pushed the throttle forward to its furthest position, bringing the small boat to its top speed. His big, calloused hands sat lightly on the wheel as he made minor adjustments to his course, instinctively responding to the smallest changes in the ocean's currents.

He glanced at the luminous numbers on his square, black watch. He had made good time in the crossing. According to his calculations, he would reach the island soon after nightfall, just as he had planned. The darkness did not concern him; he would have no problem entering the harbor and finding the mooring. Daylight or night didn't matter. He'd done it hundreds of times before. Even though the last time had been more than ten years ago, he knew that little had changed on Santa Catalina Island since then.

Little that mattered to him now, anyway. He thought he'd given up caring what happened there, left it all behind on the night he had—what, escaped?—so many years earlier. That night he had made the channel crossing back to the mainland in record time, swearing that he would never return to the island again.

But he had been wrong. Even though he stayed away, the feelings wouldn't leave him alone, not that soon, and not that easily. He had no choice but to learn to live with the hard, bitter knot of remorse and disappointment that twisted in his gut. But eventually, the years and the distance had finally done their work, until now it sometimes seemed to him as if his time on the island had been a part of someone else's life, a very long time ago.

He zipped up his windbreaker. Even now, during the late summer, it was cool out on the water after the sun dipped below the horizon. He remembered well the cold kiss of the sea-moist air against his face, the ocean's reminder of her ultimate, unalterable supremacy over the men who crossed her.

The lights of Avalon became visible through the fast-fading dusk. As night closed in, wrapping the island in darkness, little lights flickered on throughout the town rising up the hillsides surrounding the harbor. Tiny white mast lights appeared, twinkling like fireflies swaying gently over the moored boats.

When the boat reached the harbor entrance, he pulled the throttle back into neutral, letting the boat drift for a moment in the gentle current at the opening. He drank in the dark, rugged outline of the island, the warm glow of lighted houses, and finally the shimmering white of the Casino, rising in dramatic splendor, bathed in light.

The man took a deep breath, suddenly conscious

of his heart pounding in his chest. Nothing had changed. The scene he had carried in his memory for more than ten years was before him again. Chad Carver was finally home.

ONE

"Damn tourists!"

Tucker Ryan held the bicycle inner tube under the water and watched for bubbles. Sure enough, there were two, three—no, four!—tiny streams of silver bubbling up through the shallow water of the dented metal washtub. Why didn't people stay on the paved roads the way they were supposed to?

She marked the bubbling holes with chalk, and tossed the dripping black tube in the direction of her work bench. It bounced off the wall and landed on the scarred wooden surface of the bench with a wet plop. The inner tube wasn't worth the effort it would take to repair, but she didn't have the money to replace any of her shop's equipment before it was absolutely necessary.

Use it up, wear it out, make it do, or do without. She could almost hear her father's voice. Doubtless he would approve of her thrift. Although he'd been dead nearly seven years, his wealth of tart New England maxims still often came back to her, especially when she was working in her shop. Tucker Frost had spent many hours in the workroom of Frost's Fix-It, patiently teaching his daughter how to do precise work with both her hands and her mind. If he missed having a son, he never let on to anyone, and especially not to the daughter who had been named after him.

Tucker dried her hands on her worn jeans and looked around the shop in weary evaluation. The late summer sunlight flooded through the tall double doors, which were pulled open on their tracks as wide as they could go, and pooled in long golden rectangular shapes on the wooden floor. There was a lot of work to be done.

Two of her mopeds were in pieces around the shop already, one with a sticky carburetor, the other with a bent frame. And now she needed to mount a new tire on this one, or be out yet another unit on the last big weekend of the season. It looked like this would be another late night.

She didn't really have a choice; living in a resort town like Avalon meant that she, like most of the islanders, depended on the tourists for her livelihood. And that meant she had to be ready for them when they arrived. She tried to shake off her irritation, and stepped outside for a break.

Racks of bicycles and mopeds filled the small, low-fenced yard, all painted bright fire-engine red, her shop's signature color. Her spirits lifted as she saw the beautiful new sign, her biggest investment of the summer and well worth the money, which stood proudly at the entrance to her yard. It replaced the faded, hand-lettered one she had painted herself almost six years ago.

GREASED LIGHTNING. BICYCLE AND MO-PED RENTALS. Bright red letters on a shining white background overlaid her zig-zag lightning bolt logo. And in smaller letters at the bottom of the sign: Tucker P. Ryan, Owner.

She looked from the sign to her fleet of bikes, neatly racked around the perimeter of the yard— all of them gleaming in the sun, each one polished to a bright high gloss. They all passed her critical inspection. She kept her equipment in top condition, and if her bikes weren't the newest, they were always the sharpest-looking on the island. Her father would definitely have approved.

She leaned against the warm wall of the shop, enjoying the soothing feel of the sun against her skin. No matter how busy she was, Tucker always stopped for a few minutes several times each day to experience the beauty of the island. She never wanted to lose her appreciation for it. At first, she had to force herself to take time out in a busy day, but now it had become a ritual, one that she now practiced without conscious decision, an essential part of her hard-won serenity.

A growing stream of tourists passed by her yard, mostly day-trippers, laden down with cameras and souvenirs, hurrying to the dock to catch the boat back to the mainland. Parents picked up tired little children for the last few steps. Older children ran ahead and shouted encouragement back to their parents. Couples of all ages walked arm in arm, shamelessly enjoying their last few minutes on the romantic island.

A long, low whistle sounded from the waiting boat, calling all stragglers aboard. Tucker knew without checking her watch that it was 6:15. At 6:30 exactly, the boat would pull away from the dock to begin its return passage across the channel, decks filled with tired passengers waving a reluctant goodbye to Santa Catalina island.

Tucker understood exactly how the tourists felt. Only six years ago, she'd been one of them herself. She remembered the first time she had made the crossing. The trip had been a surprise for her birthday, planned with Peter's usual flair for the dramatic.

"Today," he'd announced that Saturday morning, "we leave behind the concrete and freeways, the traffic and smog of this great city of Los Angeles. If only for one day, we shall escape!" Then he swept her up in his arms and kissed her, and they both dissolved with laughter. They'd laughed a lot in those days.

Peter's adventures always delighted her, but Catalina touched her in a different way. When they arrived on the island, they discovered a rugged, unspoiled jewel that almost seemed to float suspended in another century. Tucker could hardly believe that such a place existed only twenty-six miles off the coast of Southern California, and she soon realized that their single day on the island would be far too short to even begin to see its natural wonders. The day passed quickly as they explored the island together; the storybook town of Avalon and the rugged, wild beauty of the island's interior. Far too soon, it was time to go home to the city.

When the big boat pulled slowly out of the harbor at the end of the day, returning to the mainland, Tucker watched with a feeling of regret as the lights of Avalon came on. She squeezed Peter's arm tightly as tears formed unexpectedly in her eyes. In only one day, Catalina had already stolen her heart.

"Hey, Tucker! No more daydreaming!" The husky voice startled Tucker out of her reverie. A petite red-head waved enthusiastically from the door of the bikini shop on the corner. "It's Friday night! Let's you and me stir up some action in this boring town!"

Tucker laughed and waved back. Judy could

always make her feel better. She was forty-eight, eighteen years older than Tucker, but she had the irrepressible energy of a teenager, and by her own admission, she directed most of that energy toward the pursuit of men. Judy crossed the tiny street in three quick steps.

"Come on, Tucker, we're wasting precious time! Lock up the shop, go home and get that disgusting grease out from under your fingernails. Take a nice hot shower and transform yourself into the gorgeous Ice Goddess of Avalon." Tucker smiled tolerantly at her friend's teasing name for her. "We'll knock 'em dead at the Anchorage tonight!"

Judy had a perfectly manicured hand on one tiny hip and cocked it suggestively. "And I'm definitely not interested in a lot of boring girl talk tonight, if you know what I mean, so you'd better look your best. We'll use you as bait and see what we catch."

"Are you kidding? I've got three bikes out of commission going into Labor Day. I don't want to be short of rentals on the last big weekend of the season. You know I need the money too much."

Tucker pulled her fine blond hair into a neat pony tail with one hand and searched in the pocket of her jeans for a rubber band with the other. "Besides, you certainly don't need me as bait. As a matter of fact, you don't need any help at all.

You do just fine on your own." She wrapped the rubber band around the shoulder-length flaxen twist of hair.

Judy shook her head and laughed her deep, throaty laugh. "Well, all right, I'd be lying if I didn't agree. I have to admit I do all right for an old gal."

"Judy—"

She held up a tiny hand. "I've kept myself together. Nevertheless, I would absolutely kill to have your legs." She gestured toward Tucker's long legs, hidden in workday denim. Judy touched her short-cropped red hair in an unconscious gesture of vanity. "But you're right. I still do okay." Her voice grew serious. "You, on the other hand, are too young and pretty to live like a recluse in that tiny house."

"I like my house." Tucker was instantly defiant. Judy never gave up. She could sense the conversation heading into familiar territory. Judy was a good friend, but Tucker often wished she would mind her own business.

"It's a fine house. I'm not talking about the house and you know it. A woman needs more than an empty house and a yard full of mechanical . . ." Judy fluttered a delicate hand with distaste toward the mopeds, ". . . things to make her happy. A woman has got to take care of herself. A woman needs attention. She needs to be pampered. She needs companionship. *Male* companionship, my dear Tucker. Do I have to be more explicit?''

"I'm really hoping you won't be." Tucker crossed her arms and shook her head in warning.

"Come on, Tucker. This is for your own good. The way you're living isn't right. You can't spend the rest of your life pretending you're not lonely."

"Judy, I don't want to talk about this. It's none of your business." Her tone was steely.

Judy looked as if she were going to say more, then thought better of it. When she spoke again, her voice was gentle and persuasive. "I know it's none of my business. We won't talk about that. We'll just have fun, okay? Come on, Tucker, won't you come out with me tonight? I promise you'll have a good time."

Tucker sighed. She didn't want to hurt Judy's feelings. She knew her friend was doing what she thought was best, and maybe there was even a little bit of truth in what she said, but Tucker didn't want to think about that right now.

"Honestly, Judy, I would, but I have to get these bikes running by tomorrow morning. Thanks for asking, really. I appreciate it. Maybe another night, when things have slowed down a little."

"What am I going to do with you?" Judy gave Tucker a quick hug, then held her at arm's length for a moment. She cocked a plucked and penciled eyebrow at Tucker. "You're a real challenge to me, do you realize that? It's a good thing I love you so much. So how about next Friday? Will you promise me?''

''Okay, I promise,'' Tucker agreed reluctantly. ''The season will be over then, maybe I'll have more time.''

''It's a definite date, and be warned, I'm going to hold you to it. Well, I've got to lock up the shop and run home to make myself irresistible. At my age, it takes just a little bit longer. You'll find out yourself one day. See you tomorrow, Tucker.'' In a couple of quick hops, Judy crossed the street and disappeared through the hot pink door of the Sweet Nothings Bikini Shop.

Tucker watched her go and shook her head fondly. Judy was something else. Tucker knew that behind her somewhat brassy exterior was a caring, sensitive person. She had been the first of the islanders to make her feel genuinely welcome, and Tucker would always be grateful for her kindness during that lonely and painful time. Judy had given her support and sympathy, but had respected her need for privacy as well. Gradually, they had grown into good friends, and eventually, best friends.

There was no question that Judy was fun to be with, but Tucker didn't enjoy their occasional evenings out the way that Judy did. Living on an island with exactly 2,470 permanent residents did make for a shortage of available men, but that didn't deter Judy. She had been born on the island,

and was reconciled to that situation. She jumped into each new, or renewed, relationship with both feet.

Tucker, on the other hand, didn't like fending off the same handful of single men over and over again. She had come to Catalina for comfort and solitude, not to be the belle of a very small ball.

The Ice Goddess of Avalon. Tucker's mouth formed a hard line. She knew that some of the other islanders besides Judy used that name for her behind her back, and not always kindly. Why not? She didn't really blame them. It was true. The ice was in her heart.

The fading sunlight glistened across the surface of the harbor, and gleamed on the pristine white surface of the Casino out on the point, which stood like an elegant sentinel watching over Avalon. The round Moorish-style building overlooked the harbor that sheltered boats of all sizes, from luxurious yachts to leaking dinghies.

Avalon had always evoked in Tucker the feeling of a Mediterranean seaport, at least the image she knew from books and movies, since she had never been to Europe. That was a trip she had thought she and Peter would take together some day, when there was time.

Of course, she had always thought they'd have forever. The thought stabbed briefly at her, fresh and hot. For an instant the pain was as sharp as ever, but she waited patiently, and in a few moments it slowly faded to a dull ache, and then finally left her completely.

The masts of the sailboats swayed back and forth in a gentle soothing rhythm, the boats rocking in time with the gentle wavelets of the harbor. The sun struck gold highlights on the darkening water as sunset approached. In a few minutes, the sun would slip behind the island and nightfall would begin. Tucker let herself absorb the peaceful scene for a few moments, then went back inside.

In the shop, she searched for her technical manuals on her workbench without success. She finally found them on her desk, buried under a stack of bills and invoices. She pushed the pile of paperwork to one side, first making a solemn promise to herself that she would deal with it later, and opened the tattered manual.

She would start with the carburetor problem. She had tried all the usual remedies with no success, so now it was time to try the books for another suggestion. She sat down at her battered wooden desk and turned on the lamp. It was going to be a long night.

___ TWO ___

Tucker tightened the last bolt securing the axle to the fork of the bike's frame and stepped back with a sigh. She spun the wheel briskly, carefully watching as it slowed to a stop, then spun it once more. When she had satisfied herself it was correctly balanced, she hung the wrench back up in its place on the pegboard rack above her workbench. She glanced at the battered electric clock on the far corner of the bench. Quarter past eight. She'd been at the shop since before 7:00 this morning.

Tucker stretched wearily. She had repaired the equipment she needed for the upcoming weekend, and more than anything right now she wanted to walk the six blocks up the hill to her cozy house and go straight to bed.

Tomorrow, Sunday, and Monday the town would be flooded with tourists. Between the weekend visitors from the mainland and the cruise ship passengers who would be in port, Avalon would swell to nearly four times its normal population. It would be a great luxury to have a good night's sleep to prepare for the onslaught of activity that she knew was coming.

She looked at the stacks of papers on her desk, and remembering her promise to herself earlier, shook her head. As much as she wanted to go home, she really needed to spend some time paying the shop's bills and getting her finances in order. If she didn't take care of it tonight, there would be no time again until next week, and she couldn't afford to pay late charges.

Watch the nickels and dimes, and the dollars will take care of themselves. She smiled in spite of her fatigue. *I know, Dad, I know.*

Resigned, she stifled a yawn and stretched again, then washed her hands in the basin in the corner of the shop and dried them on a scratchy blue paper towel. She poured the last cup of stale coffee into her chipped yellow mug and sat down at her desk to begin.

Chad entered the inner harbor, keeping the boat's throttle well below the wakeless speed required by Avalon's harbor patrol. He counted the rows of boats until he reached the ninth row, where no pleasure craft were moored. Turning down the row, he counted the silent commercial boats he passed until he saw the one he was looking for.

The old glass bottom boat bobbed silently at her mooring, with a tiny dinghy tied up behind her. She was a sad sight, having been neglected in the water now for more than a month. She was an old boat with a wooden hull, and had always required a lot of work. He'd poured gallons of sweat into keeping her afloat and running smoothly. Of course, he knew it was unlikely she had received any kind of decent maintenance since he left the island. The old man had always relied on him to do that, along with everything else.

Of all the places he'd worked since he left the island, he'd never worked as hard, or for less, than when he'd worked for the old man. How many hours had he spent trying to hold the business together? How many days, how many nights? He had been captain, crew, and chief mechanic when most of his friends were still playing hide-and-seek.

Countless nights he had come home exhausted, the old man nowhere to be found. Chad knew he would be parked on his regular stool at the Marlin Club for the night, talking the bartender's ear off, or, if he'd gotten an early start, he might already be passed out in his bed.

Usually there was no food in the house unless Chad had bought it himself on the way home after locking up the shop. He would make himself some instant coffee to stay awake long enough to study for school the next day.

When he was young, it was fear of the old man that had kept him going. By the time he was thirteen, it was hate. Pure, undiluted hate, and the treasured belief that someday he would be able to escape.

The faded maroon canvas stretched over the cockpit and passenger seats was white with seagull waste. The mooring lines trailed brown slime. Barnacles and green muck had already partially obscured the name on the boat's stern, but Chad didn't need to read the broad script to know what it said.

Irene. He grunted in disgust. This was all the old man had ever managed in the way of a tribute, and it had always struck Chad as a rather pathetic one at that. His memories of sanding and refinishing this old boat in the hot sun were much more vivid than his few gauzy recollections of the gentle woman it was named for. He remembered a sweet scent, a warm touch, but the woman's face was always unclear in his memory. Sometimes he couldn't remember anything about her at all.

He tied up the rented power boat behind the *Irene*, rafting onto the same mooring, and cut the engine. He turned slowly in a full circle as he evaluated the activity in the harbor. The scene looked like the beginning of every Labor Day he could remember on the island. All four hundred moorings in the inner harbor were filled, many with two boats tied up together. The harbor patrol was busy directing late arrivals to anchor in the outer harbor, which was already dotted with boats of all sizes.

On many of the larger pleasure boats, the cocktail hour was in full swing, and the breeze over the water played tricks with the sound, bringing him wisps of music, bits of conversation, and floating laughter. On a large yacht two rows over, a brilliant white light over the bridge illuminated a chic woman holding out a tall glass to her tanned escort, signaling for another gin and tonic.

The shore boat was making its rounds through the harbor, picking up and dropping off passengers going into Avalon for the evening. If he sounded his air horn, the shore boat would stop to pick him up as well, but Chad didn't feel like joining a crowd of partying tourists. He would make his return to Catalina by himself, and under his own power. He stepped cautiously into the small dinghy tied up behind the *Irene*.

He picked up the red gas can connected to the

tiny outboard and shook it. It was empty; whatever gas it had held had long ago evaporated. That didn't matter, since the condition of the motor itself was questionable, and it was only a short distance from the mooring to shore anyway. He found two oars in a tangle of rope and smelly rags on the bottom of the dinghy, and fit them carefully into the rusted oar locks. He untied the dinghy and began slowly stroking toward the lights of the shore.

A few minutes later, Chad pulled in his oars and tied up next to several dozen small rubber boats and dinghies at the ramshackle dock reserved for them. The dinghy dock floated between the immaculately maintained facilities of Catalina's two exclusive private clubs, the Tuna Club and the Catalina Island Yacht Club. He'd not been welcome at either place before, and they certainly wouldn't want him now.

He stepped up onto the worn wooden dock, which was dimly lit by the light reflected off the Casino a hundred yards to the right. Now only the short length of the dock separated him from the island he had been away from for so long. Still he waited, prolonging the moment, absorbing the sight of Avalon before him. Several couples strolled along Crescent Avenue, the street that curved gently along the narrow beach at the harbor's edge.

Chad walked slowly up the uneven ramp and

reached street level. As he started up the board-walk, confusion suddenly washed over him in a disorienting wave. He slowed his pace, then stopped completely. He lost some of the confidence in his memory he'd felt while on the water. The scene before him was now both familiar and strange to him, like a jigsaw puzzle with a couple of extra pieces that wouldn't quite fit, or home movies with strangers in the background.

Where did that pink building come from? Something else had been there before, he was sure. The Pleasure Pier seemed farther from the dinghy dock than he remembered. And what had happened to the tallest palm tree that had marked the exact middle of the town beach, the one he had carved his name into one summer night when was twelve? He scanned the beach until he located it, but it was no longer the tallest; another tree reached higher now.

Only the smell of the island was exactly as he remembered; a blend of cool, salt air and warm, dry earth that he would recognize no matter how many years and miles distant he might be from Catalina. He closed his eyes and inhaled deeply.

The scent carried him back to his childhood, a blur of memories of late nights spent working in the shop and long afternoons on the water. When he opened his eyes, it was as if Avalon had shifted slightly and dropped back into its old familiar place. The earlier feeling of disorientation left him. All was familiar again.

Chad walked slowly along the boardwalk that connected Casino point to downtown Avalon. When he reached Crescent Avenue, he walked more quickly through the busy tourist section of town, where crowds of people overflowed from the restaurants and bars out into the street. He passed quickly through the Island Plaza area, staying close to the beach and as far out of the light as he could, then he slowed his walk again. Soon he came to the quiet corner where he would turn to start up the hill to the house. He stopped and waited, looking up the darkened street. He was only a few blocks away now.

Other, darker memories crowded his mind: the back of his father's hand on his face and the taste of blood in his mouth; his back sunburned and aching from work; the terrible darkness of his bedroom closet. Some of the details were blurred together by the kind wash of time, but the pain was still sharp and fresh and new.

A cool breeze was starting to blow off the water. One of the big boats in the outer harbor sounded its low, mournful horn twice, and the sound reverberated deep in his gut.

The image of a small boy, alone in a house without lights, forced itself into his consciousness with astonishing clarity. He could hear the boy's crying in his mind, a small, animal-like sound of despair. The sound in his head grew louder and louder until, mercifully, the boat sounded its horn again and drowned out the sound of the child's sobbing. He pushed the memory of the boy out of his mind.

Chad made his decision. He didn't want to face the house just yet. He needed some more time. *As if ten years haven't been long enough*, he thought. Tonight it didn't seem to matter. Ten years or a hundred, he still wasn't ready to go back there.

Maybe before going up to the house he'd stop at the old workshop. That was a good idea. He would see what kind of shape the shop and yard were in, then he could take a look at the house. That would be easier. He zipped up his dark blue windbreaker and started walking.

Tucker worked quickly, and in half an hour she had written out checks for most of the shop's regular monthly expenses and recorded them in her ledger—utilities, insurance, the payment on the equipment loan she had taken out when she started the business. Thank goodness that was almost paid off—only four more payments. She had been lucky to get it, even though the interest rate was astronomically high.

The last check she wrote was for the rent on the shop and yard; Tucker searched her desk for the new address. Her landlord, Joshua Carver, had died suddenly two months ago. Since then, she'd been sending her rent to the attorney who was handling his estate.

It was too bad about Joshua, Tucker thought as she wrote out the check. A ruddy-faced, white-haired man, he was the owner and captain of the oldest glass bottom boat on the island, the *Irene*, named after his late wife. For more than thirty years he'd taken tourists out to see the marine life that flourished in the clear water surrounding Catalina, and to hear his stories of the island's early days. Although the newer boats with their young captains and slick patter captured most of the business, a trip on the *Irene* featured something that none of the new boats could offer: Joshua's stories of the island from a real old-timer's perspective.

"Some of my stories are true, and some of 'em might just be fish stories," he would always tell his passengers as they pulled away from the dock. "It's up to you folks to decide which is which!"

Tucker smiled at the memory. Joshua Carver had treated her like a kindly grandfather from the day they'd met. In six years he had never raised the rent on the shop, even though she knew he had passed up several opportunities to replace her with a more profitable tenant. He was a good man, and although she didn't know him well, when she heard the news of his fatal heart attack, she was sincerely saddened.

Tucker slipped the last check into its envelope and sealed it shut. She stamped the envelopes and stacked them neatly in the middle of her desk so she'd remember to give them to Forrest, her mailman, in the morning. She touched the stack lightly for a moment. She was getting by.

Yes, another month gone, and things were still tight, not as bad as a few years ago, of course, but it was always a juggling act. This summer season had been the best she'd ever had, but she still needed every dollar that the holiday weekend would bring.

Not so very long ago she remembered going to bed at night with the burden of her financial worries eclipsed only by the ache of her loneliness and sorrow. God, how she had missed Peter. In many ways, she missed him just as much now, but she had become used to the pain, so she felt it less. It hadn't been easy. But she was getting by. The thought both comforted her and saddened her.

Tucker stood and rubbed her tired eyes. The light from the desk lamp cast high shadows against the wall, and reflected glaringly back from the window opposite her desk, turning its surface into a silver mirror. Tucker jumped at the face in the glass, nearly knocking over her chair, then smiled ruefully back at it as she recognized her own reflection. Her heartbeat slowly returned to normal.

Time to go home and get some rest, she thought. *You're getting a little skittish, jumping at shadows.* She opened her top desk drawer and found her big ring of keys, then clicked off the lamp.

At the moment she put out the light, a strong sensation flooded her body. She was not alone. Someone was there with her. Someone was watching her.

Her heart beat fast again, but strangely, she felt no fear. She stood in the darkness for a long minute, listening for anything out of the ordinary, but all she heard was the distant rumbling of the surf. The familiar sound was comforting. She was imagining things.

Calm down, she told herself firmly, *you're just a little jumpy*. She jingled her keys to fill the shop's silence and walked to the door with quick, deliberate steps.

Chad stepped back into the shadows as the window went dark. The image of the woman disappeared, but he could easily follow her path to the door by the sound of her keys. The front door to the shop opened and shut. The deadbolt turned with a solid click. A few seconds later, footsteps crossed the yard, and he recognized the squeak of the gate opening.

He took a silent step forward, but was careful to remain within the shadow of the structure. The woman closed the low gate behind her, then turned back. She hesitated. Something had caught her attention again.

Chad leaned back further into the shadows, praying she couldn't see him. *Damn it, Carver*, he thought, *it'll serve you right if she sees you and starts screaming. Then for damn sure you'll have some explaining to do.* He held his breath.

How had he ended up in this situation? He hadn't meant to spy on this woman, whoever she was, but once he'd caught sight of her in the lighted window he hadn't been able to break away. He didn't know for sure how long he'd been standing there in the dark, watching her at her desk, head slightly inclined as she concentrated on her work.

Now as she stood at the gate, her face was nearly as visible to him in the bright moonlight as it had been earlier in the artificial light of the shop. Her fine blond hair spilled out like a halo over the hood of her dark sweatshirt. She was tall, and the cool elegance of her face was an odd contrast to her jeans and shapeless sweatshirt. But what held him transfixed were her eyes.

They were gray, shimmering and deep, filled with some lingering emotion he couldn't quite read. If he wasn't so worried about being discovered, he'd be tempted to take a step closer to try to read the secrets those eyes held, but of course, he couldn't risk it. It was clear she was on alert for any sound. He waited. A trickle of sweat ran down between his shoulder blades.

The woman tilted her head slightly, listening, then turned away with a little shake of her head, apparently satisfied there was nothing amiss. She closed the padlock on the gate with a sharp snap, and slowly surveyed the yard one more time. Then she turned and started walking up the hill with a long graceful stride, her hands shoved in the pockets of her sweatshirt.

Chad watched the woman from the shadows until she turned right at the top of the hill and disappeared. He walked around to the side of the shop and admired the dozens of red bikes standing ready, shining in the moonlight. He imagined the woman polishing them to this high gloss, her hair brilliant gold and white in the summer sun. He saw her kneeling down to check the tension on a chain. For the first time since he'd arrived on the island, he felt the oppressive weight of his past lift slightly.

He stood looking at the well-kept yard until a cloud passed over the moon and shadowed it in darkness. He took the opportunity to scramble over the fence, landing softly on his feet on the other side, his tautly muscled legs absorbing the impact.

Chad walked back around to the street and

started walking back to the intersection where he'd stopped earlier. This time he paused for only a moment before he started up the hill. It was time to go home.

THREE

  "Tucker, I'm telling you, you should have seen the look on his face!" Judy was inside her shop making coffee, but her brassy voice carried easily to the bench in front where Tucker waited.

The two of them started most summer mornings this way, with coffee and conversation on the small wooden deck in front of Sweet Nothings at 7:00 a.m., usually a full hour before the earliest island visitors were up and about. Tucker loved this time of the morning, watching Catalina wake up to another beautiful day. From Judy's deck she could see not only the harbor and the Casino, but the hillsides of Avalon, dotted with brilliant splotches of colorful bougainvilleas and tall eucalyptus trees. It was one of her favorite views of the island.

Judy emerged with two steaming coffee mugs, her cigarette case and lighter, and settled down on the bench. She handed Tucker her coffee and continued her story without missing a beat.

"I wish I'd had my camera!" She lit one of her long thin cigarettes and blew smoke out in a dramatic cloud. "I've never seen that exact expression on any man's face before."

"Now who was it, again?" Tucker waved the smoke away with a weary gesture. Judy had a habit of starting every story somewhere in the middle, and filling in all the details as she went.

"Buddy Thompson, from the harbor patrol. I told you! We used to go together years ago, when I was young and stupid." Judy reflected briefly. "Well, actually, I guess it was really a couple of different times, as a matter of fact. Aren't you listening?"

"Sorry." Tucker tried to make herself pay attention to Judy's rambling story. Usually she found Judy's retelling of her escapades entertaining, but this morning she was preoccupied with her own thoughts.

"Anyway, Buddy was sitting at the bar when I came in, which was a total surprise to me. He certainly never took me any place that nice when we were together. Naturally I pretended not to notice him, and sat down at one of the little tables by the window. You know, looking out over the water." Judy took another drag on her cigarette, enjoying her own story immensely.

"Well, pretty soon I feel these hands on my shoulders, sort of massaging them. Buddy says 'Alone tonight, Judy?' and I say 'No, as a matter of fact, I'm meeting someone and please take your hands off me.' I don't even look up at him. I'm very cool. But Buddy keeps massaging my shoulders and says in this creepy voice, 'You used to like this, that's what I remember. You liked it a lot.' And I say, 'Well, I used to like drinking Ripple until I tasted champagne,' and I reached back and stabbed my swizzle stick right in that jerk's hand." Judy brayed with triumphant laughter.

"Isn't that priceless? I swear, that man's ego is the biggest part of—Tucker, what is wrong with you today? You're awfully quiet this morning."

"It's probably nothing, Judy, but—" Tucker fidgeted with her sunglasses, deciding whether or not to confide in her friend. "Something kind of strange happened at the shop last night, and I can't keep from thinking about it. It just keeps coming back to me."

"Honey, what happened? Tell me." Judy rubbed a smudge of her pink lipstick off the rim of her coffee mug.

"I had to work late, like I told you, and when I was finished and was getting ready to leave, I had a very strange feeling. I felt like someone was outside, watching me.''

''Watching you? You mean like a Peeping Tom?'' Judy's eyes glistened with excitement. ''What do you mean? What happened? Were you scared?''

''No, that was the strangest part. I felt him watching me, first in the shop and then again when I was leaving, but for some reason I didn't feel like I was in danger, or really even frightened at all.''

''Him! A man, naturally. So you got a look at him! What did he look like? Tall? Short? Fat?'' Judy was bouncing with intensity. ''Did you call the police?''

''No, I didn't see anything, or even hear anything, really. It was just a feeling. I'm afraid the police wouldn't have taken me very seriously.''

''A feeling? You didn't actually see anything at all?'' Judy seemed disappointed.

''No, I told you, it was just a strange feeling. But I'm absolutely certain someone was there.'' Now Tucker was embarrassed she had told Judy, but the memory of the sensation she'd experienced had been so strong, she had felt compelled to tell her.

''Sounds like a ghost story to me.'' Judy opened her red satin case and felt inside for another cigarette. ''Hey, that's it; I know who it was!'' She pulled out the cigarette and laughed in triumph.

"Who?" Tucker asked warily.

Judy looked around with elaborate caution. "It's the ghost of Joshua Carver, that's who was watching you."

"Judy, come on. Don't be ridiculous." Tucker was really sorry she'd confided in her now. "Joshua was a wonderful old man and I don't like you making jokes about him now that he's passed away."

"I'm not joking. I suppose you probably don't believe in ghosts?" Judy kicked off her sandals and stretched her legs out in front of her and admired her brightly painted toenails.

"No, I don't, and I should be getting to work." Tucker put her coffee mug down on the bench with a clunk.

"Tucker, you shouldn't be so closed minded. It's a well-known fact that if a person dies with unfinished business from this life, his spirit may return to walk the earth, unable to find his eternal rest," Judy said, simply and sincerely, as if she were stating that the sky was blue.

"Judy," Tucker said with a sigh, "I think you've read too many Shirley MacLaine books."

"Laugh if you want, but everyone in this town knows that Joshua Carver died of a broken heart, and that's absolute fact. If anybody had good reason to have a restless spirit, he would for sure."

"What do you mean? I know his wife died quite a few years ago; he told me that," said Tucker.

"He talked about her sometimes. I always got the feeling that he still really missed her, even after all this time."

"Losing his wife wasn't the end of that poor man's troubles. His son was another heartbreak." Judy shook her head and clucked her tongue.

Tucker was surprised. "I didn't know he had children. He never mentioned any." How much did she really know about Joshua? Against her will, Tucker was being drawn into Judy's story.

"Just one, a son. Cutest little boy you ever saw. He was only eight or nine years old when Irene Carver died." Judy took a long drag on her cigarette. She blew out the smoke and studied the cloud thoughtfully. "Now, I guess I'm really showing my age here, since this all happened more than twenty years ago, but I still remember everything quite clearly. I was in high school then."

"What happened?" Tucker was intrigued in spite of her skepticism.

"Well, Irene and Joshua did almost everything together, I remember that. They really seemed to be in love. He was a few years older than she was, but everybody said it didn't matter, they made a good pair. They liked to take a walk together early, nearly every morning, when it was barely light. Days when it was warm enough, they'd go for a quick swim in the ocean, too. Usually they'd leave the little boy asleep in bed, but this morning he woke up with a stomach ache. Joshua volunteered to stay home with him while Irene went for her walk.''

''And what happened to her?''

''When she didn't come back, Joshua got worried. He called a neighbor to look after the boy and went out looking for her. He found her body on the rocks of Lovers' Cove, where they usually went swimming. Apparently she'd hit her head on a rock underwater and drowned. No reason for it. It was just one of those things that happens. Kind of a freak accident.''

Tucker felt a twist of remembered pain in her chest that brought a flood of empathy for the old man's loss. *Just one of those things. Like Peter. It could have happened to anyone, but it didn't; it happened to Peter.*

''How horrible for Joshua, and the little boy, too.''

''Joshua just about went crazy with grief. He blamed himself, said he never should have let her go by herself, that if he'd been there it wouldn't have happened. Which might have been true. Who knows?''

Judy stubbed out her cigarette with her delicate fingers. ''Joshua got drunk, and stayed drunk for a couple of weeks as I remember, but who could blame him? Another family had to take care of the little boy until Joshua was able to pull himself together and go on.''

''And he never remarried?''

"No, he raised the boy all alone. When the boy was older he helped out on Joshua's boat quite a bit. I think he was always quite a handful."

"You said that was just the beginning of his troubles. What else happened?"

"Well, I don't know the rest of this first-hand. I was living over at Two Harbors at the time, but my sister always kept me up-to-date on what was going on here. That's when I was married to Kenny. You remember, I told you about that. Biggest mistake of my life. What a rat *he* was."

Tucker nodded, impatient. "Yes, you told me. But what happened to Mr. Carver?"

"Anyway, I guess Joshua devoted himself to taking care of his son, and being both father and mother to him. You know it must have been hard for him, but he always put his son first. Pretty much sacrificed everything for him. When the boy was finished with high school Joshua sent him off to college on the mainland, even though money was tight. And how do you suppose the kid repaid his father for his love and support?"

"How?"

"On one of his trips back home to the island, he got this girl he'd been seeing pregnant. When he found out about the baby, he dumped her and completely disappeared."

"Disappeared? What do you mean?"

"After his father found out about the situation, they had quite a fight. Joshua begged him to do the honorable thing, offered to lend him money, let them live with him, whatever he needed. But the kid wouldn't have any of it. He left the island and never came back. Never even spoke to his father again. Literally packed his bags and left in the middle of the night. At least that's the way I heard the story.''

''That's terrible. What happened to the girl?''

''Nobody knows. She left the island right after he did. She'd been working as a cocktail waitress at that dive that burned down a couple of years back. She didn't have any family here on the island. She had only been living here about a year; nobody really knew anything much about her or where she'd come from before.''

''And Joshua never saw his son again?''

''Not once since it happened, and that was more than ten years ago. So you can see what I meant when I said that Joshua probably died of a broken heart.''

Tucker felt her sadness for the old man grow deeper. Her own suffering, safely locked away from the everyday world, came rushing back painfully fresh, as it always did when she heard about someone else's loss. Yet despite what Judy said, Tucker knew it was not possible for anyone to die from a broken heart. If it were, she knew she would be dead herself.

FOUR

"Hey, Tucker, it looks like you've got your first customer of the day already."

Judy's voice brought Tucker back to the present. She looked up from her cold coffee.

Across the street near the entrance to her yard was a lean blond man in blue nylon running shorts and a gray sweatshirt. He was tall, and he was walking with long strides up and down the sidewalk in front of Greased Lightning, head down and breathing deeply. He looked as if he were cooling down from an early morning run. Tucker wondered why she hadn't seen or heard him approach.

A large dark arc of moisture stained his shirt over his back and shoulders, and streaked the front in broad vertical bands. He shook a fine mist from his thick hair with a powerful toss, like some big predatory cat, then swiped the dampness from his eyes with the back of a thick wrist.

He stopped his pacing and slowly bent over in a stretch, taking hold of his taut calves for a few deep breaths. The long muscles of his legs tensed and rippled; then he rolled up gradually, an inch at a time, each vertebrae on his back outlined against the damp fabric of his shirt, until he stood upright and stretched his arms toward the blue morning sky.

Tucker felt as if she were watching some powerful animal in the wild, confident of his place in his natural habitat, unaware that he was being observed. She felt a shiver of guilt about watching him like this, but she did not look away.

The man peeled off the sweatshirt in a fluid, easy motion, and tied it around his waist. His damp T-shirt clung to the hard planes of his upper body. He pulled it up to wipe the sweat from his face and neck, exposing a tanned, flat abdomen.

"Mmm, nice. Very, very nice." Judy made a little growling sound of appreciation low in her throat. "If you aren't going to help him this very minute, Tucker, then maybe I will go over and see what he'd like. You know how important it is to make our visitors feel welcome." She laughed wickedly.

"Very funny, Judy. He doesn't look like he's

interested in renting anything. I'm sure he's probably just stopped here to—'' The man stretched again, then strolled into the yard full of shining red bikes. After looking around curiously for a moment, he walked deliberately to the window where Tucker helped her customers. He leaned his forearms on the counter and peered into the shadowy interior of the shop.

Judy threw her a pointed glance.

''Well, all right. I'll go see what he wants. He probably just needs directions or something like that.'' Tucker put down her half-empty coffee mug. She noticed her hand was shaking slightly.

''Honey, he doesn't look to me like the kind of man that would need *directions* at all. I'd bet he already knows where everything is; all the important things anyway.'' Judy laughed again, and this time the man turned and looked toward them, as if he'd heard everything they'd said.

''Oh, great. Thanks a lot, Judy.'' Tucker's voice dropped to a whisper. ''Now he thinks we've been staring at him all this time.''

''Which is exactly what we've been doing,'' Judy answered in a loud stage-whisper. ''And, no matter what you say, I certainly intend to keep right on doing it.''

The man's gaze met Tucker's and held it. She felt her cheeks grow suddenly warm with embarrassment, but she was unable to look away. The feeling of his eyes on her was definitely unsettling.

She had the sudden sensation that he knew some secret about her, or had a bit of confidential knowledge that gave him an unfair advantage.

She was used to dealing with strangers: families, women, children, and yes, single men, too; she did it all day long. She had the diplomacy and tact learned by years of handling a steady stream of demanding strangers. And on those occasions when tact failed, she didn't have a problem with telling an overly aggressive man to get out of her shop and leave her alone. So what was disturbing her about this man? Why did she hesitate to cross the street and find out what he wanted?

Now he was facing outward toward her, leaning back against the center on his elbows, his hips and powerful legs thrust forward in an attitude of arrogant relaxation. His gaze was unwavering. He was clearly waiting for her, and she felt as if she were moving much too slowly, but she couldn't make herself go any faster.

Tucker waved awkwardly. "I'll be right there," she called out with forced cheerfulness. She turned back to Judy, who was watching with a smug smile. "See you later, Judy." She put a friendly customer-service smile on her face and crossed the street back to the shop. Her legs felt wobbly underneath her. She willed herself to walk faster.

Chad watched her approach, and marveled at the easy, graceful quality she brought to simple movement. She was wearing a short-sleeved teal blouse and white cotton shorts with sneakers. Her bare legs were long and tan, just the way he'd imagined they'd be when he had seen her in jeans last night. She was wearing her hair loose, and it skimmed her shoulders in a shimmering fine cloud of white gold. He imagined how it would feel under his fingers—like some rare silk, smooth and fragrant.

He had not planned on coming here this morning. Last night, the first night in his father's house, had been a tough one. Old memories had followed him from room to room like Marley's ghost. Ten years had not been enough to blot out the scenes from his past that each room held. Sleep was elusive in his old bedroom, and he'd eventually given up and moved to the big couch in the living room.

He'd changed position dozens of times on the lumpy couch searching for sleep, thoughts of his father and his old life in Avalon close and real and ugly in the night. Comfort had finally come when he had let himself think about this woman, the unknown woman of the boat house he had unintentionally spied on earlier in the evening. Something about his memory of her was peaceful and comforting. Chad let himself think of her, only of her, and sleep had finally taken him.

This morning, when he awakened, it had not been with the nightmares of the past he so often had, but instead with a vivid image of this woman, an image of her tawny skin and secret places that had stirred a hot need within him.

What had branded the thought of her into his brain? She was beautiful; but the past ten years had brought him plenty of beautiful women. As a dive guide in some of the world's most famous resorts, he had never had a shortage of female attention. Whenever he had wanted them, there were always lovely, willing women who had found him a pleasant vacation diversion, just as he had found them convenient distractions. No messy relationships. No hard feelings. No lies. He preferred it that way.

But he didn't have time for this woman, even if she did have eyes that a man could lose himself in, and a body that begged to be caressed. He couldn't deny that he'd been imagining what it would be like to make love to her since the moment he had first seen her, to see those eyes flicker with pleasure.

But that didn't matter. He was here to finish the old man's business and be rid of his memory for good. The sooner he was off this island, the better.

So he had made this morning's run extra long and punishing to work the uncomfortable ache of desire from his body. He wouldn't let himself be distracted. He pounded out mile after mile on the road leading up to the ridgeline, then doubled back to the series of hills that edged the backside of town. He ran until his calves ached and the heavy muscles of his thighs trembled with fatigue. Yet, miles later, his course had still brought him here without planning; almost without conscious thought.

"Hi, can I help you?" Tucker met the stranger's eyes without flinching. The man looked her up and down slowly, not bothering to hide his frank admiration. His eyes were somewhere between green and blue, framed by thick blond lashes almost white at the tips. The heat of his gaze sent a warm flush over her skin.

"Do you want a bike for the day? Or maybe a moped, since it looks as if you've already had your exercise. I've got a couple available, but most of them are already reserved."

The man's face was youthful, but his features were too powerfully defined to be called boyish. He was deeply tanned, with high cheekbones and a strong, straight nose. An arrogant, sensual mouth was curved in a slight smile. His hair was an unruly mass of dark blond, bleached lighter in streaks by the sun and slightly curly across his forehead and at the nape of his neck. Something in his eyes was older than the rest of him, a darkness that she couldn't decipher.

Tucker waited for him to speak, the unsettled feeling in her stomach growing stronger by the moment. When he didn't answer right away, she continued, more sharply than she'd intended, "So what do you need?"

The man nodded toward the sign. "Greased

Lightning.'' He smiled, revealing a flash of white teeth and crinkling the corners of his eyes. ''Good name.'' His voice was deep, and somewhat ragged, as if he hadn't spoken yet this morning. ''I don't need a bike. Thanks anyway.''

So what are you here for? Tucker thought, but she said nothing. The man had claimed his spot against the counter with a relaxed authority that suggested he would stay just as long as it suited him.

He shifted his weight, but kept his position, elbows against the counter, lean hips forward. Tucker guessed that when he stood up straight he was probably six feet two inches, maybe a little taller. His breathing had slowed to normal, his chest and abdomen rising and falling with a slow, steady motion. She followed the movement with her eyes.

Inexplicably, Tucker felt a little rattled. She kept talking to fill up the silence. ''Is this your first time on Catalina? I can recommend some good tours.'' Her face felt warmer, and the flush spread down her neck to warm the skin exposed at the top of her blouse. ''The Casino tour is great, and so is the inland motor tour, if you have enough time; it takes about four hours, but you can really see a whole lot of the island.'' Damn it, why didn't he stop leaning against her counter that way?

''Thanks, but I've spent quite a bit of time here.

I can find my way around pretty well.'' He smiled again, and a hint of mischief glistened in his eyes. ''So you must be . . .'' He checked the sign again. ''Tucker P. Ryan?'' He cocked a bushy blond eyebrow at her quizzically.

She nodded. ''That's me.''

''If you don't mind me asking, where did you get a name like Tucker?''

She didn't take offense. She was used to the question, even from total strangers, although coming from this man the familiarity was unnerving. She repeated the story more quickly than usual. ''It's a family name for the firstborn. It was my father's name, and my grandfather's name, and my great grandfather's name. When I came along, it was the first time the firstborn had been a girl, as far back as anyone could remember anyway.''

''But your parents stuck with the family tradition. I think that's great.'' He crossed his legs at the ankle, and the edge of his shorts pulled up slightly, straining over the muscles of his thighs.

''Well, they were expecting a boy, but my father said he wouldn't mind sharing his name with me anyway.''

''So what's the 'P' for?''

''Priscilla.''

''You've got to be kidding.'' His thick brows popped up in surprise. ''I'm sorry, you're not kidding. You're serious.''

''That's okay, don't worry about it. Believe me,

I feel the same way. That was my mother's idea. She said if my father wanted to go through with calling me Tucker, she thought I deserved at least one really feminine name. She meant well, but, really—Priscilla?''

He stood up straight and stretched again, and she mentally measured him against her five-feet-eight-inch frame. The man was even bigger than she had first guessed—tall, and very solid. He smiled again, a quick sexy flash of startling white against his tan.

"I think you'd better stick with Tucker. It suits you," he said, stepping into the open doorway of the shop to look in. "You've done a great job fixing up the old boat shop. It's a big improvement."

"Look, I don't mean to be rude, but do I know you?" she asked, although she knew she didn't. She recognized many of the island's regular visitors, at least by sight, just as she knew their boats moored in the harbor. But she was certain she had never seen this man before.

"No. I just remember this building, that's all."

He turned around to face her, and the easy mischief she had seen earlier had vanished, replaced by something darker in his eyes. "I'm sorry, I don't mean to be rude. My name's Chad." He extended a hand. She shook it awkwardly. His large palm was warm and dry, his fingers long and work-roughened.

"Well, Chad, I know you haven't been here for quite a while, because it hasn't been the boat shop for at least six years. I've had the lease that long." She was puzzled. Tucker was used to dealing with two classes of people: tourists and islanders. Each person she spoke to every day fit into one of those two groups. This man didn't. He wasn't a local, but he certainly wasn't the average island visitor here for the day or the weekend.

"Well, I guess things do change, even on Catalina. I used to think that nothing ever changed here." The ragged edge of his voice had smoothed out a bit, but it still had a rough, smoky quality that made Tucker think he was not a man who wasted a lot of words.

"Yes, they do change," said Tucker, "but not much, and not fast. People here are pretty attached to things the way they've always been."

"When I was a kid, I remember I once asked my dad why the Casino was always painted white." Chad jerked his thumb over his shoulder in the general direction of the majestic circular structure on the opposite side of the harbor. "I told him it was boring. I thought maybe they should try painting it some other color for awhile. I was very fond of purple at the time, as I recall."

"What did he say?"

"He wasn't amused. He said that white had been good enough for Mr. Wrigley in 1929, and so it had just better be good enough for me."

Tucker leaned against the warm wall of the shop. The early morning sun was climbing higher, and she had things to do to prepare for the day, but in spite of that, she found herself intrigued by this man. She knew that very soon their privacy would be shattered by the arrival of the passengers of the big boat. Already the harbor was waking up with activity.

"How come you know so much about the island? Most folks who visit here never see much beyond Avalon, or maybe they make it up to Two Harbors if they've got their own boat. Quite a few people seem to think Catalina is just another place to go out to dinner and drink too much."

He pressed his lips together into a hard, thoughtful line for a moment before he answered. "I was born here."

"Really?" Most people that Tucker knew who were born on Catalina never dreamed of leaving. Even a relative newcomer like herself couldn't imagine living anywhere else now.

"Yes, I grew up here. But I've been away a long time." The darkness she had seen earlier clouded his eyes again.

"Does your family still live here? Maybe I know them. I've only been here six years myself, but you know it's like a small town. Everybody pretty much knows everybody."

"No," he answered sharply. Then, almost apologetically, "they're all gone now." For a few

awkward seconds, Tucker felt like she had somehow put her foot firmly into her mouth, although
she wasn't sure why.

Chad pushed aside the memories that Tucker
had unknowingly stirred up. He didn't want to
think about the past. He didn't want to think about
all the crap he should be sorting through and packing up back at the old man's house right now. He
wanted to think about today. He wanted to think
about Tucker P. Ryan. He smiled, using all the
charm he could summon.

"What are you doing tonight?" For some reason he couldn't yet articulate, he didn't want to
let this woman go. "Maybe we could have dinner,
and you could fill me in on what's been happening
on the island for the last couple of years. All the
local news and gossip. Tell me if anybody's been
campaigning to paint the Casino purple."

Tucker got the empty feeling in her stomach,
the one she always got when something like this
happened. "No, I don't think that would be a
good idea." The Ice Goddess of Avalon. She
heard the name in her head. Why did saying no
to a man always make her feel like she ought to
apologize, like there was something wrong with
her? "I mean, this is going to be a very busy
weekend for me. You know how the last weekend
of the season is here." The excuse sounded hollow
and false even as she said the words.

"Sure, that's okay. Don't worry about it. I

know how it is." Chad looked at her, for the moment put off. He knew when he was being brushed off. He wasn't used to forcing his attentions on a woman. It wasn't his way, but he didn't want to give up. He was deciding how to proceed when something inside the shop caught his eye.

"Who's the diver?" He gestured toward Tucker's scuba equipment stored neatly against the side wall of the shop. Her well-worn BC vest and wetsuit hung on hooks, her tank and weight belt stacked on the floor beneath. "Is that your equipment, or does it belong to someone else?"

"It's mine." Tucker felt he was really asking another question. What was going through his mind right now? "I don't get to go diving as often as I'd like, especially during this time of year, but I go as often as I can."

"Have you ever been to Starlight Beach?" His eyes glowed with some memory she could only guess at. "That was one of my old favorite spots."

"No, but I know the name. That's pretty far, almost to Land's End, isn't it?"

"That's right. Just about a mile short of there. It's a beautiful place; nice beach, excellent visibility. You can only get there by boat, so it's very secluded, and I think the diving there is about the best on the island. Or at least it used to be."

"I don't have my own boat, so I haven't been diving that far west." She was distracted by the rattle of the gate opening to admit her first customers of the day.

An overweight woman in a lime green dress entered the yard, towed by a little boy about ten, who dropped her hand and began running up and down between the rows of bikes. A teenaged couple strolled in, arms locked lovingly around each other's waist. Two men in funny long shorts carrying maps stopped on the sidewalk outside the gate and began arguing in a foreign language.

"Looks like my day is starting." She was suddenly grateful for the interruption. "It was nice talking to you, Chad. I've got to get to work."

"Let's go diving." His gaze was direct, unwavering. The sudden statement flustered her for a moment, then she found her voice.

"Now? Very funny." She gestured at the growing crowd of customers.

"No, not today. Next week. Tuesday. Take the day off." He looked at the activity on the street and in the yard and smiled knowingly. "Something tells me that after this weekend is over, you'll have earned it. We'll take my boat and I'll show you Starlight Beach."

"I don't know . . . I mean, I couldn't close the shop . . . I'll have to . . ."

"I need a bike for my little boy." The large woman planted herself between Tucker and Chad. "Which one of you is going to help me?"

"I'll be right with you." Tucker went behind the counter and found her clipboard. She searched for a pen. "Chad, thanks for the offer, but I don't think—"

"I don't want a stupid bike! That's for babies! I want one of these mopeds!"

"I'm sorry, you have to be at least sixteen for the mopeds. You can have lots of fun with a bike." Tucker smiled apologetically, and looked to the mother, who didn't appear to be terribly concerned about her son's behavior, for support.

The little boy kicked the ground furiously, raising a cloud of dust as he glared defiantly up at Tucker. She silently began counting to ten. Chad was right. When this was over, she really would need a day off. Chad was still standing there, patiently waiting for her response, a little half-smile playing over his lips.

"Okay. Let's go." She could scarcely believe the words were out of her mouth, but it was too late now. She didn't even know this man! What was she doing?

Chad gave her no time to reconsider her decision. "I'll pick you up here Tuesday morning at 6:30." He surveyed the busy yard, now crowded with more people.

The woman in the lime green dress was trying in vain to soothe her angry son. The teenage couple was leaning against the wall of the shop, kissing passionately, oblivious to all else around them.

The foreign men were joined by their wives and marched in toward the counter, waving their guidebooks in front of them with grim determination.

"Chad, maybe that isn't such a good idea. I have a lot of work to do, and I don't think—" Tucker was cut off by the little boy's shrill voice.

"Give me my *moped*! I want it *now*!"

Chad smiled knowingly at Tucker. "Don't worry. Just bring yourself and your gear. I'll take care of the rest." He smiled again, and with a cheerful wave of his hand, he trotted out the gate and down Crescent Avenue toward the Casino.

FIVE

On Tuesday morning, Tucker woke up at 5:15, fifteen minutes before her alarm clock. To her surprise, she was wide awake and rested. Last night she had been bone tired at the end of the three busiest days she could remember since she had opened Greased Lightning. Although she was grateful for the business, she was exhausted. What had she been thinking when she agreed to a dive trip this early in the morning, especially the day after Labor Day?

Of course, she thought as she poured herself a bowl of cornflakes and non-fat milk, that really wasn't the big question. The big question was what she was doing going on this trip at all? She stared into her bowl as if she expected to find some answer there.

Judy had practically danced in celebration when she heard the news. She had come over early Saturday evening after closing up Sweet Nothings and demanded to know every detail of Tucker's conversation with the man she had dubbed the Mysterious Stranger.

"I can't believe it! You, Tucker Ryan, have a date! Not a set-up, not a blind date, but a real date with the most gorgeous man I have seen in years!" She hugged Tucker with embarrassing enthusiasm and started her dance of joy again.

"Judy, please, you're embarrassing me. First of all, it's not a date. We are going scuba diving together, which is, believe me, about the least romantic sport in existence." Tucker returned to the task of checking her dive equipment. . . her BC for leaks, her regulator for proper air flow. "If you had ever seen what a person looks like right after a dive, you would understand. It's not the kind of thing you can look your best doing."

"Well, maybe you're right about that part of it," said Judy. She fingered the rubber wet suit with a distasteful grimace. "This would not be terribly flattering to any woman's figure. You'd certainly never see it in my shop." Judy crossed her arms over her petite chest, unwilling to give up. "But you are going alone, right? Just you and the Mysterious Stranger?"

"Yes, I guess so." Tucker was already nervous about this trip, without Judy's inquisition. "I mean, he didn't mention anyone else."

"And where did he promise to whisk you away to?"

Tucker checked the straps on her fins. "Starlight Beach." One was cracked and starting to tear, so she searched her gear bag for a replacement.

Judy clapped her hands triumphantly. "Alone with a Mysterious Stranger on Starlight Beach. Now *that* sounds romantic to me, no matter what you say."

Tucker finished her cornflakes, and rinsed her bowl and spoon in the sink. Judy was always pushing her toward one man or another. What Judy didn't know was that Chad had been on her mind since Friday, in spite of how busy she had been over the three-day weekend.

In her mind she had replayed their conversation over and over, trying to recall exactly how she had agreed to see him this morning, but much of their meeting was now a blur in her mind. Spending a morning alone on a boat with a man she had met only once was not in her comfort zone. But for some reason, she had said yes. Something about him had struck a chord of recognition within her. Maybe that was why she had agreed to go diving with him.

But that wasn't enough to overcome her nervousness. Since Peter, she had rarely even been alone with a man. The few times she had ventured out on a date had been nothing but depressing. It was simply easier for her to be alone. But this morning wasn't like that anyway: it wasn't a date; it was a dive trip. So why did she feel so unsettled?

She put the dishes in the rack by the sink to dry and checked the clock again—6:00. Chad wasn't meeting her at Greased Lightning until 6:30. She might as well have another cup of coffee.

As she was pouring it, she remembered that she didn't have a dive knife for the trip. She had lost hers on her last dive at the beginning of the summer. There was one packed in Peter's things. She hesitated, deciding if she would rather do without than have to look. It would be a necessity if the dive sight had kelp. She made her decision.

She went to the closet in the small second bedroom and pulled out a sturdy medium-size cardboard box. It still had her address written across the top in black marker. She had shipped it over from the mainland when she moved out of their old apartment in Los Angeles six years ago.

Tucker opened it. It was an odd collection of items. Most of Peter's few belongings she had given away, but there were some things she hadn't been able to part with, not because of any great significance or value, but because they reminded her so vividly of him.

Packed on top was a faded gray hooded sweatshirt, Peter's favorite. She touched the soft cotton for a moment, lost in memory. She held it to her cheek, then put it aside. She searched among the few other items: his undergraduate degree in the maroon leather folder, a battered canvas briefcase, the cufflinks she had given him on their wedding day.

The dive knife was at the bottom of the box in its black rubber case, straps wrapped neatly around it, his name handwritten carefully in waterproof paint. P. RYAN. Peter had always loved diving; he had started when he was a teenager. He had insisted that Tucker learn so they could go together.

She laid the knife on the floor beside her and slowly began to pack the other things away.

She missed Peter desperately, and she knew that in some ways she was still grieving for him. But sometimes she thought she missed other things even more than the time they had spent together. She missed the things they had never had, the events they had never shared—the children they had planned and hoped for, the retirement they had joked about. More than anything, she missed the future. Tucker missed the future that had been stolen from both of them.

She gently placed the old sweatshirt in the top of the box and folded the crinkly tissue paper over it. Tucker had learned how long she could spend remembering before she would lose control and slip back into grief. She did not want to give up her memories, but she could not let them control her life now. That had been a lesson dearly learned. She closed the box and slid it back into its place in the closet and shut the door.

Tucker returned to the kitchen; it was 6:15. She finished her coffee in a couple of quick gulps and put the mug in the sink. She tucked the dive knife in its case in her purse, lifted her keys from the hook by the back door and started walking the six blocks to her shop.

Chad was waiting at the gate when she arrived. He was wearing navy blue sweat pants and a windbreaker. He was bigger than she remembered him, and his eyes were hidden behind dark sunglasses. Tucker felt a sudden twist of panic in her stomach. What was she doing? She had only met this man once. And where had he been for the last three days? She didn't even know where he was staying.

"You're right on time." He smiled, and pushed his sunglasses up on top of his head, revealing his eyes. His expression was one of pure happiness at seeing her, and Tucker felt some of her uneasiness about the morning begin to fade away. "I expected you to be dragging a little after the weekend you've had. Maybe we should have planned on a later start."

"That's okay. It was a really crazy three days, but I only live a few blocks from here, right up the hill, so I didn't have to get up too early this morning." She unlocked the shop and retrieved her equipment, which was all neatly stowed in her gear bag. "Besides, I'm looking forward to diving. I haven't been for a couple of months." She locked the door and put a large red CLOSED sign on the shuttered window.

"I'll carry this for you." Chad picked up her gear bag as easily as if it were empty, slinging the wide black strap over a broad shoulder. "My stuff is already in the boat. I got a couple of full tanks at the Dive Station first thing this morning, so I think we're ready."

"I guess so." They walked to the end of the pier where a small powerboat was tied up. A tiny dinghy was secured bottom-up on the fore deck. Chad stepped in first with Tucker's gear bag, which he stowed in the hold under the fore deck, then offered his hand to help her step in.

The boat pitched slightly as she stepped down, and she lost her footing, falling against Chad. His body was warm and solid beneath his thin windbreaker. She steadied herself with her free hand against his chest. Under her palm she felt the movement of fluid muscle. Her heart was pounding, and she felt a sudden weakness in her legs that scared her.

"Whoa, are you okay?" Instantly, Chad had wrapped his arm around her shoulders, steadying her against his body. She felt strength in his hands, but he held her gently, as if he were afraid of hurting her. He looked down into her face, which was only inches from his own. His eyes searched her face with concern.

"I'm—I'm fine, I just lost my footing for a second." Tucker straightened up and Chad slowly removed his protective arm from around her. She felt her face burning. "Guess I haven't got my sea legs yet." She sat down on the padded seat and willed her heart to slow its beating.

"Getting the passengers safely in and out is always the hardest part." Chad cast off the lines securing the boat to the pier, then slipped behind the wheel and started the engine.

He was glad for the distraction of the activity. The warmth of Tucker's body pressed against him, if only for a few seconds, had ignited the need for her that he had been carrying within him since he had seen her through the window that first night. His body's response to Tucker had been immediate and powerful, a sudden rush of blood to his loins that had caught him unaware. He felt like he was sixteen years old again, at the mercy of his hormones. Blushing beneath his tan, he silently gritted his teeth and concentrated on getting safely out of the harbor.

Tucker watched Chad as he eased the boat smoothly away from the pier. Coming out of Avalon Bay, he accelerated and headed west. The boat was surprisingly fast for its size, and Tucker began to relax as they skimmed along the calm ocean.

Chad's thick blond hair was blowing in the wind, and a wide smile lit up his features. He yelled over the roar of the motor, "Great day for diving!"

Tucker smiled and nodded. It was too difficult to talk over the sound of the engine. To her left the island's coastline revealed cove after cove, large and small, most with a few boats moored within their protection. The sea was a deep blue-green, and the sun was quickly taking the morning chill from the salt air.

They approached the narrowest section of the island, Two Harbors, or as most of the islanders called it, the Isthmus. Tucker remembered that when approaching Catalina from a distance, this point appeared to divide the island into two peaks of land rather than one. Only when you got much closer could you see that Catalina was really only one island.

She had been diving as far west as the Isthmus, but not for years. In fact, the last time she had been diving at Two Harbors was with Peter, on their honeymoon. The memory of the day they had spent there leapt vividly into her mind as they passed Bird Rock, rest stop for flocks of sea gulls, cormorants and brown pelicans.

Tucker remembered sitting with Peter on the boat between dives, laughing and holding hands. Peter had made a game of talking back to the sea birds, squawking and sputtering at them, and it seemed as if they understood him and squawked

right back. Peter could always make her laugh.
She smiled at the memory, which, though tinged
with sadness, still amused her.

The coastline was less familiar now, and Chad
slowed the boat down and stood to survey it as he
cut in closer to the land. He pointed to the broad
beach bounded by grassy hillsides. "That's Emer-
ald Bay. Good visibility there, too. Not much farther to go now." He smiled at Tucker. "I promise
I'll make it worth having to get up so early in the
morning."

"It's been worth it already." To her surprise,
Tucker found Chad easy to be with. She didn't
make friends easily, and it seemed as if men in
particular always wanted to push her into something she didn't want. Ever since Peter, she had
usually found it easier to avoid them altogether.
But Chad had a relaxed manner that put her at
ease. Something about him touched her in a way
she couldn't quite put her finger on—something
that had kept her thinking about him during the
last hectic three days. She was glad she had said
yes to this trip.

A few minutes later, they reached Starlight
Beach. The cove was empty this morning, not sur-
prising due to its remote position on the island.
No other boats were on the few permanent moorings in the transparent waters, and no campers
were visible on the beach, a small, perfect wedge
of sand nestled at the base of steep, rugged cliffs.

Chad put the engine into neutral and moved quickly to the bow of the boat. He released the anchor, then returned to the wheel, turning the boat into the current until the anchor caught firmly in a sandy patch on the bottom. He cut the engine, and the morning air was suddenly silent. The boat drifted in the slight current, pulling the anchor line taut.

Chad stood, took a deep breath, and stretched tall. His body was a long line of dark blue against the deep blue green of the water. He unzipped his windbreaker and tossed it aside, then turned and gestured expansively toward the cove. "Well, what do you think?"

"It's beautiful." Tucker hesitated a moment, listening. "And it's so quiet!" She smiled. "I think that's the best part."

"You're right, but just wait until we get down there," Chad pointed to the crystal waters beneath them. "That will be even better." He quickly shed his sweat pants and pulled off his T-shirt, revealing a broad chest tapering to a narrow waist. He was deeply tanned, and the breadth of his chest was covered with sun-bleached blond curls that formed a golden path down to the waistband of his trimly cut trunks.

"Let me have your gear. I'll get it set up for you." Chad took her bag and unzipped it. He pulled a tank from the hold between the seats and began to connect Tucker's equipment to it. The muscles in his back rippled smoothly as he moved the tank close to him, trapping it securely between his knees.

Tucker realized she was staring, and she felt a flood of color rush to her cheeks. She quickly looked away, and slipped out of her jeans and hooded sweatshirt. It felt strangely intimate to be taking off her clothes so casually with Chad only a few feet away, even if underneath she was wearing her black no-nonsense one-piece swimsuit.

Chad was finished with her equipment and he was now setting up his own. Although he appeared to be giving his full attention to the gear, Tucker felt an awareness of her body, a feeling that he was watching her. It gave her a fluttery feeling low in her stomach.

Tucker began pulling on her wetsuit. Although the water would be warm at the surface, it was often quite cold underneath, even at shallow depths. She left the top unzipped so she wouldn't become overheated in the warm morning sun before they entered the water.

Chad finished with the gear and slipped into his wetsuit. He passed Tucker her weight belt, and lifted the tank and vest for her to put on. He handed her mask and fins to her. "Let's enter off the back."

By the time Tucker had positioned herself at the rear of the boat with her mask and fins on, Chad had easily slipped into his own gear and was right behind her. "Let me turn you on," said Chad. He adjusted the valve on her tank to that position.

"After you," Chad gestured toward the water as if he were opening a door for her.

"Okay." Tucker put one hand on her mask and stepped off the stern of the boat.

She was surrounded by the familiar splash of blue and white as she entered the clear water of the cove. She drew her first breath of air and adjusted the seal of her mask. She checked the fit of her vest and weight belt. When she was confident that all was well, she let a bit of air out of her vest and descended to ten feet to wait for Chad.

The surface of the water above her shimmered like a mirror, broken only by the underside of the boat which was clearly visible above and to the right of where she waited. She looked around, surveying the conditions of the site. Visibility was excellent, as Chad had promised. She estimated nearly sixty feet. Depth where they had dropped anchor was about forty feet. Below her was a reef that fingered out into several smaller reefs, creating a wealth of crevices to explore.

Chad entered the water with a splash of bubbles. Tucker watched as he checked his equipment, then looked around for her. He caught sight of her and held out his hand with thumb and forefinger touching, using divers' sign language to ask, "Are you okay?"

Tucker nodded and responded with her own okay sign. With a couple of kicks of her fins, she was at Chad's side. He took her hand, and together they began their slow descent to the bottom of the cove. As they made their way down, she shivered slightly at the dramatic change in water temperature. The thermocline was quite noticeable, and she was grateful she had worn her full wetsuit.

The reef was teeming with life. Although Tucker had spent many hours diving many of the more remote locations surrounding Catalina, she couldn't remember ever diving a sight as pristine as this. It was as if they were the first two humans to have visited this spot.

Tucker let Chad take the lead, and they began their exploration of the reef. A school of bright orange garibaldi welcomed them, a pretty but common sight in these waters. Chad moved quite slowly, with an easy confidence. Tucker felt very relaxed, much more so than she usually did during a dive, and she felt as if she were seeing things that she might have missed at her ordinary pace. She was amazed at the wide variety of tiny reef fishes she saw—some she was familiar with, and some she had never seen before. Delicate sea fans waved in the current in hues of mauve and purple. Anemones reached out from the rocks, pulling in unwary prey.

Chad stopped and waited for a moment, suspended over the reef. He motioned to Tucker to come close to him, and when she did, he pointed to a crack in the rocks. Tucker looked, but saw nothing. She looked quizzically at Chad. He pointed again. Tucker followed the direction of his finger, and this time she saw peering out from the crack the ugly leering face of a moray eel. Although she knew it was not dangerous unless provoked, she shivered at the sight of it, knowing that its teeth could inflict serious damage to the unwary diver's hand. She was glad when Chad moved on.

When Chad stopped again, it was for a gentler creature. An octopus was perched on top of a rocky outcropping, virtually invisible due to its protective coloring. Chad carefully caught the shy creature by allowing it to swim away freely, but holding his own palm in front of it. The octopus gently bumped against Chad's hand, propelling itself forward with a graceful swish of its tentacles. Before it could become distressed, he removed his hand and let it escape.

Tucker was pleased with Chad's reverence for the undersea creatures. Too many times she had been diving with people who carelessly damaged the underwater world, clumsy human intruders into a perfect ecosystem. Chad seemed to understand that they were only visitors to this world; it was not theirs to disturb.

Chad checked his watch and pressure gauge. He

signaled to Tucker that they had used up the safe time for their dive; it was time to get back to the boat. Tucker checked her own watch in surprise; the time had passed so quickly that she hadn't realized how near the end of the dive they were. She followed Chad as he led them back to the boat, and they slowly made their ascent to the surface.

Chad climbed the ladder into the boat first, shrugged off his equipment in a corner, then returned to the ladder to help Tucker into the boat. He took her equipment from her shoulders, and stowed it safely away with his own.

"Well?" Chad's eyes matched the intense blue-green of the water from which they had just emerged. "What did you think?"

"Chad, it was incredible!" Tucker pulled the damp strands of her hair away from her face. "I could have stayed down all day."

"Me, too. I'm in the water nearly every day, and the world down there is still just as amazing to me as it was the first time." Chad unzipped the front of his wetsuit, exposing a wedge of tan skin from his neck to his waist.

"Every day? What do you mean?"

"I do this for a living. I'm a dive guide."

"You're very good. I should have guessed. Where do you work?"

"Up until last month, I was in the Virgin Islands. Before that, Cabo San Lucas, Honduras, and Hawaii. Oh, and a couple of months in Belize.''

''Sounds like you've moved around a lot. Why?''

Chad shrugged. ''I get restless. Besides, there's too much of the world to see.''

''What about Catalina?''

Chad shook his head. ''No, there was never time.'' He slicked his hair back from his face. ''You know what would be perfect after a dive like that?''

''What?''

''How about breakfast?'' Chad's eyes glistened with mischief.

''Sounds great, but it's a long way back to Avalon. It'll probably be lunchtime by the time we get back.''

Chad pulled a cooler from the hold. ''I took the liberty of packing a few things. I thought breakfast on the beach would be a good idea.''

''It's a great idea.'' Tucker began to tug out of her wetsuit. Chad scrambled to the fore deck where a large black bag was suspended.

''But first, how about a fresh water rinse? It's warm.''

''A solar shower? You think of everything.'' Tucker peeled her wetsuit off. Chad held the black bag aloft and offered her the showerhead. Tucker rinsed the salt from her long legs and body, then began on her hair.

"Here, let me do that." Chad took the showerhead from her. Tucker tilted her head back, and Chad directed the stream of water into her hair. Warm, fresh water ran through her shoulder-length hair and over her neck and shoulders. Chad reached out and lifted the heavy mass of hair from her shoulder and sprayed the nape of her neck. She rolled her head back in a luxurious gesture of relaxation. She closed her eyes and Chad rinsed her face as she tilted it up toward the summer sun.

"Thanks. That was heavenly. Let me hold it for you." Tucker took the bag as Chad stripped his wetsuit off. He took the showerhead from her and rinsed his torso. Water sluiced down the hard planes of his chest and trickled down his abdomen. His body glistened in the sun. He quickly finished his shower as the water supply in the bag trickled to an end.

The sun was high in the sky now, and soon they were both nearly dry. Chad flipped the dinghy into the water, and stepped into it with the cooler and a blanket. He offered his hand and Tucker followed him into the tiny boat. With only a few powerful strokes of the oars, they reached the beach. Chad dragged the dinghy up onto the sand.

With a flourish, Chad spread the bright cotton blanket on the sand and put the cooler next to it. They settled themselves down on the smooth surface, which was warm from the sand beneath it. In order to share the blanket, they sat close together, both facing out toward the clear waters of the cove. Tucker took a deep breath, enjoying the peaceful solitude of the beach, at the same moment strongly aware of Chad's presence so near her.

Chad opened the cooler. "Breakfast is served." He extracted a basket of strawberries and a crinkly white bag. He opened the bag and offered it to Tucker. "Baked fresh this morning." She reached in and chose a croissant.

"Chad, this is just beautiful!" She bit into the croissant. It had a sweet, buttery flavor, light and flaky. She brushed a crumb from the corner of her mouth. "I thought stale crackers and oranges were always the rule after a dive."

"That's for the average dive excursion. I wanted this trip to be special." He offered her one of the plump, red strawberries. She bit into it, and the juice exploded sweetly, a trickle escaping from the corner of her mouth. Before she could reach it, Chad carefully brushed it away with his thumb.

He reached into the cooler and extracted a bottle of champagne and two plastic glasses. He tore off the foil and popped the cork with a deft twist, poured a glass and passed it to Tucker, then poured one for himself. "It's a celebration."

"What are we celebrating?"

"Three things. The end of another summer season for Greased Lightning, for one thing."

"Amen to that. I don't care if I ever see another tourist." They touched glasses in a toast.

"My finally making it back to Catalina, for another." They toasted again.

"What's the third?"

"Meeting you." Chad tapped their glasses together a final time.

Tucker tasted the champagne. The sensation of hundreds of tiny bubbles was delightful as it slipped down her throat. She drank more quickly than she intended, and the popping bubbles tickled her nose. She looked over the rim of her glass at Chad. He was watching her, unsmiling, his champagne untouched. He put the glass aside, on top of the cooler, never taking his eyes from her.

Chad leaned toward her and took her in his arms, drawing her to him with a movement of rough need, crushing her against him. Her nearly empty glass fell from her hand unnoticed. His bare chest against her breasts was warm, warm as the late morning sun on her back. Her nipples tingled with pleasure at the sudden pressure of his body against hers, with only the thin fabric of her swimsuit between them.

Tucker's heart was racing, but she didn't resist. She didn't want to resist. Something was happening that had been set in motion the first moment Chad's eyes had locked onto hers back at the shop. It was as if they had been moving toward this moment, slowly, imperceptibly, but inevitably, since they had met. It felt good. It felt right.

Chad's hand was at the back of her neck, guiding her to him. His mouth found hers, firm lips seeking soft. His mouth crushed against hers, and almost without conscious thought, she parted her lips to welcome him in. His mouth was warm and salty, an earthy masculine essence that was both foreign and familiar. She began a tentative exploration that drew a heightened response from Chad's probing tongue.

His arms held her tightly to his powerful torso, and her fingers spread out against the breadth of his back, hard muscle moving beneath smooth skin. It felt good to touch him. Suddenly, the muscles in his back stiffened, and he groaned deep in his chest, a rumbling sound that mixed both desire and disappointment. He gently broke their kiss, and pulled back.

"Chad, what is it? What's wrong?" As she spoke the words, Tucker suddenly became conscious of a sound that had been in the background of her mind for several minutes, but that she had easily ignored.

"Look." Chad gestured toward the cove, where two power boats, each laden with sunburned parents and rambunctious kids, were preparing to drop anchor. "I knew this was too good to be true."

"I guess so." Tucker's disappointment was

tinged with a feeling of relief. She had not been prepared for the effect that Chad had on her. Her heart was still beating fast, and her lips felt swollen with his kisses. She was grateful for the interruption, now that it had come. Things were happening fast, much too fast. "Maybe we should head back."

"Okay." Chad packed up what remained of their breakfast into the cooler. Tucker stood up and folded the blanket.

Chad dragged the dinghy out into waist-deep water, and boosted Tucker into it with a powerful lift. He pulled it into deeper water, then climbed in himself. Tucker watched as he dipped the oars into the water for the short distance back to the boat. She watched his shoulders work with each stroke, moving muscles that had been underneath her fingers only minutes ago.

They unloaded the dinghy and secured it on the fore deck, working together in a comfortable silence, speaking only when necessary. In a short time, Chad had everything stowed for the trip and pulled up the anchor. He started the engine, and slowly motored out of the cove.

They paused for a moment at the mouth of the cove, looking back at Starlight Beach. Where they had eaten their breakfast picnic was now the sight of a wild game of Frisbee among five children. Chad smiled ruefully at Tucker. "So much for paradise."

Tucker smiled and laughed nervously. "I guess there are still a few visitors left on the island." Chad smiled, put on his sunglasses, and pushed the accelerator to full throttle.

The trip back to Avalon passed quickly. They didn't try to talk over the engine noise. Tucker watched the coastline speed by, and wondered what would have happened on the beach if the two families hadn't arrived. Before long, the red-tiled roof of the Casino came into view.

Chad slowed the boat down as they entered Avalon Bay. "We'll tie up at the pier and unload our gear, then I'll take the boat back to its mooring."

Tucker found her shoes and slipped them on. Her dive equipment would have to be rinsed, but she decided to put it in her gear bag to make unloading and carrying easier. She gathered her mask, fins and dive booties, and disconnected her regulator and BC from the empty tank. She was zipping up her gear bag when she noticed Chad's gear bag next to his equipment.

Written on the side of his bag, in big, black waterproof letters was the name Chad Carver. Tucker stared at it for a full minute, absorbing its meaning, unwilling to believe what was now obvious.

Her mind was a blur of facts. Joshua Carver had one son. Chad's interest in the old boat house.

His long absence from the island. His sudden return. Chad was Joshua Carver's son.

Tucker settled back down in her seat as Chad guided the boat toward the pier. The sorry story she had heard from Judy was replaying in her mind: Chad deserting his pregnant girlfriend; Chad leaving his widowed father to die alone. What kind of a man would do those things?

Not the man she thought she was beginning to know, the man who had treated the octopus so gently, the man who had kissed her on the beach earlier today. But one thing was for certain: Chad was Joshua's son, and Joshua was dead.

They reached the pier, and Chad tied the boat up in the loading area. He grabbed Tucker's bag and tossed it carefully up onto the pier.

"Why don't you wait for me here while I— Tucker, is something wrong?" Chad looked curiously at her. She could see her distress reflected back in his eyes.

"I'm okay. Chad, I'm sorry, I didn't know. I just realized who you are. I saw your name on your bag. I knew Joshua—your father."

Chad's face became an expressionless mask. What was that mask hiding? Grief? Regret? Or was it simply anger at being found out?

Tucker took a deep breath, choosing her words carefully. It would be unfair for her to judge him. "Anyway, I just wanted to tell you how sorry I am about your loss. He was a good man, and I—''

"It was no loss, believe me." Chad's voice was icy, a frightening, detached tone she had never heard before.

"What? What did you say?" Tucker didn't want to believe what she was hearing.

"I said, it was no loss." He said it slowly, as if to make sure she understood him. His eyes were cold, like the cold, clear water of the cove at Starlight Beach. "And I don't need your sympathy, or anybody else's, so you can just save it. That old bastard wasn't worth anybody's tears."

Tucker stood still for a few silent seconds, then stepped up onto the dock. She picked up her gear bag. The strap of the webbing bit into her shoulder. She looked at Chad, who stared back defiantly as if challenging her to say more.

They stood that way for a long minute. Tucker swallowed, her mouth suddenly dry. "I'm sorry you feel that way, Chad. I think I had better go home. Thanks for taking me diving." She turned and started walking toward town.

SIX

For a day off, Tucker thought as she stretched the clean sheets over her mattress, this has sure turned into one lousy day.

After leaving Chad standing silently on the dock, she had spent the rest of the day doing chores at home. First she had meticulously rinsed her dive gear and left it on the porch to dry. Then, after changing into her oldest pair of jeans and tying her hair back with a bandanna, she had swept every inch of the hardwood floor of her compact house, dusted everything with a vengeance, and stripped the sheets off her bed.

Usually housework and home chores had to wait until after her work at the shop, but she had planned on taking this whole day off anyway, so she might as well use it for something. *Maybe housework is cheap therapy*, she thought as she made up her bed with fresh sheets. Unfortunately, in spite of her cleaning frenzy, she still wasn't feeling any better. If only she could make her mind as neat and orderly as her house. She shook her pillow into a clean pillowcase with a bright yellow daisy pattern.

Images of Chad dominated her thoughts: Chad at the wheel of the boat, wind blowing in his thick hair; Chad kissing her on the beach; Chad's eyes like ice as he spoke of his father's death.

She spread the handmade quilt over the bed and smoothed the wrinkles away. She stood up straight and took a deep breath, inspecting the bedroom. Everything was to her satisfaction, so she moved on, walking slowly from room to room.

By now Tucker had cleaned every surface of her house, and her mind was still fogged, so she decided to tackle fixing the slowly dripping faucet in her kitchen that had been annoying her for over a month. Since water was scarce on the island, she had been catching every drop in a bucket, using it to water her house plants, and had put off repairing the problem until business slowed down.

As she wrestled with the heavy pipe wrench, the events of the morning replayed in her mind. How could she have been so stupid? She was always so careful to avoid involvement. It was just better for her, she had decided long ago. Peter had been the proverbial one in a million, the one for her. Now he was gone, and there wouldn't be another like him. Of course she was lonely, but she was better off alone now, with her memories of him.

Chad Carver was unquestionable proof of that. The first time she disobeyed her best instincts she ended up attracted to a man who had deserted a woman when she had most needed him, abandoned the child he had fathered, and treated his own father like dirt. She certainly wouldn't expect to be treated any better. She had been a fool to let things ever get started with him.

When she had the faucet in pieces, Tucker pulled out and briefly examined the slimy, decaying washer, then tossed it in the trash. She replaced it with a new one from her toolbox and reassembled the fixture. She turned the water supply back on and tested the faucet, turning the stream off and on. This time, no drip. She was grimly triumphant. Usually she found a certain comfort in fixing broken things; there was something so tangible about it. Sometimes it even made her feel a bit more in control of her life.

A forceful knock at the door interrupted her as she was gathering her tools. She went to the door, a sense of foreboding closing in on her. When she opened the door, Chad was standing on her porch, his body a hard outline in the dusky light of early evening. He was in worn jeans and his windbreaker. His mouth was bordered with lines of fatigue, and his eyes had faint dark circles beneath them.

"I've been thinking about you all day." His voice was low, charged with simmering emotion, under control for now, but very close to boiling over. Tucker suddenly realized he was a man who could be dangerous. A small pocket of fear formed in her stomach, cold and tight.

Chad shoved his hands into the pockets of his jacket and swayed back and forth on his heels several times. Damn, but she was beautiful—even now, when she looked like he had caught her in the middle of changing the oil on one of her blasted bikes or some damn thing, with her hair tied up in a faded blue bandanna and a smudge of dirt across her forehead. He was sure he had known more beautiful women, but right now he couldn't remember who any of them were. What would she do if he took her in his arms right now and claimed her honeyed mouth with his?

Chad cleared his throat. "I'm sorry." He wanted to say more, but his mind was suddenly blank.

"You don't owe me an apology. You don't owe me anything. I don't know why you're here."

Her voice was cool and even, and he felt the contempt underneath it. The woman was absolutely right, he didn't owe her anything. He should leave her alone, finish what had to be done with the old man's things and get the hell off the island—head for someplace far away, maybe back down to Mexico. His past was none of her business, but for reasons he didn't fully comprehend himself, he still wanted her to understand. The memory of the sweetness of her mouth returned to him with agonizing clarity. He put the memory from his mind so he could try to think straight.

He inhaled slowly and tried again. "I'm here because I wanted to see you again. I didn't like the way things ended between us this morning." Chad watched carefully for any sign of regret from Tucker, but found none. "Look, I'm sorry I didn't tell you I was Joshua's son. I would have told you eventually. I wasn't trying to lie to you; I just didn't think it was that important."

"Your father was a good man, and he was very kind to me when I needed help." Her eyes softened with memories of some old pain. Chad wondered what had happened to cause the hurt he read in her eyes. "I will always remember him."

"I hated him." The words came out reflexively, unbidden, too quickly for Chad to stop them. He instantly regretted speaking, but it was too late. The words hung in the air between them like a dank fog.

Tucker felt the chilling truth behind the brief sentence. She struggled to remain calm. "Your feelings toward him have nothing to do with me, but I don't want to see you again." She began to close the door. "Please leave me alone."

"Wait a minute." Chad stopped the arc of the closing door with his hand. The door shook with the force of the solid impact. He wedged his body partway into the open doorway. "You didn't really know my father. You never lived with him. You don't know what it was like. You never knew the real Joshua Carver."

"I don't think that's the problem. The problem isn't your father; it's you. He's gone now, God rest his soul. It's you I didn't know the truth about, not him."

"What do you mean?"

"I don't think we should be having this conversation."

"I have a right to know why you're shutting me out." Chad's eyes burned with the intensity of his emotion, but what exactly that emotion was she could only guess at.

Tucker considered closing the door in Chad's face and locking it, but his hand gripped the door frame so tightly his knuckles whitened. She felt again the warning flutter of fear in her stomach.

"All right. I'll tell you. I know the reason you had to leave Catalina."

Chad's eyes narrowed to slits of shuttered emotion. "What do you mean?"

Tucker ignored the feeling in her stomach. "I said, I know why you had to leave the island."

"I don't know what the hell you're talking about. I didn't have to leave; I chose to leave. And the only one besides me who knows why I left was the old man, and now he's dead. But that doesn't matter anyway. Now it's nobody else's business but mine."

Tucker's temper flared, white hot. "Did the girl you left behind feel the same way? Did she figure it wasn't any of her business, either?" The words tumbled out in a furious tide of accusation. She wasn't able to stop them. "What about her baby? I guess it wasn't the baby's business either?"

"What the hell are you talking about?" Chad looked as if she had started speaking another language.

"Look, I think you'd better leave right now." Tucker tried again to close the door, but Chad's large frame was solidly blocking it.

"I'm not going anywhere until you tell me what you've been hearing about me." The angry set of his mouth convinced her he meant what he said.

Tucker's resolve strengthened within her. She had gone this far already. If he insisted on knowing, she would tell him. He would know that she wouldn't be taken in by his lies. She lifted her chin defiantly.

"You left the island because your girlfriend was pregnant. Your father begged you to stay, to face up to your responsibilities, offered to help you out with money, anything you needed. But you just took off. You deserted the girl, and your baby. Nobody knew where you went. Your father never heard from you again.''

Shock and confusion struggled in Chad's expression. He appeared to have no idea what she was talking about. Then understanding seemed to burst upon his face, followed by outrage. A pulsing vein of anger throbbed in his temple, but when he spoke, his voice was deathly calm.

''It's a lie. A damn small town lie, that's all it is.'' He looked into Tucker's face with hot eyes that searched and evaluated. Whatever he found in her face seemed to only confirm his icy rage. ''But no different from all the other lies, I guess.''

Chad spun around and stepped off her porch in two long steps. His long, even stride carried him down the street at a pace that Tucker knew she would have to trot to keep up with. She waited in silence, half afraid he might turn around and say something, half hoping that he would. But he kept walking, and Tucker watched him until he turned the corner at the bottom of the street and disappeared out of sight. She stood in the open doorway a minute longer, then stepped back inside and locked the door beyond her.

She was suddenly very tired. It had been a long day, and she had been on an emotional roller coaster ever since she woke up this morning. How could one day with Chad Carver have so disturbed her, so shaken her emotional equilibrium? She had worked hard to achieve some degree of peace in her life, and now one day with a man who was virtually a stranger had knocked her flat.

She went to her bedroom and took off her clothes. She stepped into a hot shower to wash away the dust and the salt that remained in her hair from the dive this morning.

This morning. The memory of their brief time on the beach together ran through her mind, images she couldn't wash away with the sand and the salt.

Chad's bare skin, golden and smooth and warm under her fingers. The pressure of his solid torso against her breasts. His mouth on hers, hungry, searching, needing, and her need answering his own with a passion that had both thrilled and shocked her.

Tucker stepped out of the shower and toweled herself dry. She put on her worn terrycloth robe and dried her hair, then slipped on a cool cotton nightgown. She eased her bedroom window open another inch. The night air flowed in, cool and tangy, the smell of the sea and the earth blended together in a fragrance that was both familiar and exotic.

She slipped between the cool, fresh sheets she had put on the bed this afternoon, and clicked off the light on the small table beside the bed. An oval pool of moonlight appeared on the shiny wood floor.

In spite of her fatigue, Tucker couldn't get comfortable. She tried sleeping on one side, then switched to the other. Her mind was a blur of memories of the last few days, and conjectures about the past. She had thought she was getting to know Chad, and then when the truth hit, another, darker version of him materialized.

But now, the image she couldn't get out of her mind was Chad's face when she confronted him this evening. Shock, yes, but disbelief, too. As if he were surprised, even baffled by her words. Lies, he had called them.

Lies. Tucker tried to find a position she could sleep in. It was hard to believe that any man could fake the emotion she had seen on his face when she confronted him. But if what Judy had told her had been lies, then what was the truth behind Chad Carver?

Several sleepless hours later, she was no closer to discovering the truth.

SEVEN

The note was not rude. Businesslike, yes, perhaps even curt, but not rude. That didn't matter. After reading those few lines, Tucker was as angry as she could ever remember being in her entire life.

She arrived at the shop at 7:00 a.m., depressed and a little bleary-eyed from her restless night. There was no sign of Judy across the street yet, which didn't surprise her. After the summer season was over, Judy usually didn't bother opening her store until noon, and by October 1st, she would only be open on the weekends.

Tucker found the plain white envelope taped to the front door of her shop, her full name typed in black, but no address. She was too tired to think much of it, and didn't bother opening it until she had turned on the overhead fluorescent lights, unlocked and opened the double doors, and put her purse away in the bottom drawer of her desk. After she started the coffee dripping, she remembered the letter. She tore open the envelope and read the few sentences.

Several seconds ticked by, before the full meaning of the words hit her like a punch in the stomach. For an instant she was stunned; then she was furious.

Dear Ms. Ryan,

Please be advised that I am in the process of liquidating the assets of Joshua Carver's estate. I regret to inform you that the property where your shop is located will be sold as part of the settlement of the estate.

Please consider this your notice to vacate the premises at the end of the month, as provided for in your lease. I am sorry for any inconvenience this may cause you.

Sincerely,
Chad Carver

Tucker read the note twice without showing any reaction, then suddenly kicked the dented metal trashcan beside her desk with such force that it rolled out the double doors with a raucous clatter.

"Damn!" She swore simultaneously at the pain

in her toes and her heart. Even after Joshua's death, she had never considered the possibility of having to move her business. Her location was ideal, but even more important than that, she had been able to afford it. From the very beginning, Joshua had rented the place to her for substantially less money than he could have gotten from another tenant. He had always said it was because he believed in her. She knew that even if another suitable building were available, she would never be able to afford the prices in the current market.

Tucker sat down at her desk chair to think, but was almost immediately on her feet again, pacing and fuming. Who did Chad Carver think he was, anyway? Was this some kind of sick revenge for what had happened between them yesterday? If he wanted to raise the rent, fine, that was understandable, that was certainly within his rights. She would pay more if she had to. She would work it out somehow. But he couldn't kick her out of the shop without any warning. He couldn't do this to her, and she would tell him so right now.

The note carried no indication of where he was staying, but Tucker had a solid hunch she knew where to find him. She locked up the shop in a silent rage, locked the gate to the yard and headed up the hill toward the house that Joshua Carver had built for his wife nearly forty years ago.

Chad heard the soft chime of the doorbell, followed at once by sharp knocking. He was in his father's cluttered office, where he had been gradually sifting through his father's records since before dawn. His back ached and he had slept badly, thinking about Tucker. He finished taping shut the cardboard box he was now hunched over, while the knocking became louder and more impatient. He smoothed the length of brown tape down on the box and straightened up. The knocking continued.

When he got to the front door, he jerked it open, irritated by the visitor's insistence. Tucker was standing on the porch, fist raised to pound on the door again. Her eyes were glowing with fierce anger, yet somehow she was still beautiful and tempting. Chad said nothing, but he felt his gut tighten in response to her. He stepped back, and she stepped into the room, not waiting to be invited.

"What the hell does this mean?" Tucker held in her hand the note he had written and delivered late the night before. She waved the page directly under his nose in a gesture of angry defiance.

Chad stopped the gesture, grabbing her wrist, his long fingers easily encircling her slender wrist. Her skin was cool and smooth under his fingers. He looked directly into her eyes as he took the note from her with his other hand and let her pull her hand away. He glanced at the note, then looked back to her before he spoke.

"Looks pretty clear to me."

His eyes slipped down her face, to her slender body, stiff with tension. Images of her as she looked on the boat yesterday morning came rushing back to him in quick succession: her eyes dancing with delight over what she'd seen in Starlight Cove; her hands pulling the damp strands of her hair away from her face; her body slick and wet as he rinsed her under the shower. Immediately, he felt a responsive tightening in his loins. He pushed the thoughts away, forcing himself back to the issue at hand.

"It means exactly what it says. I need to sell the place. You need to move out."

Tucker ran her fingers back through her hair, pulling it away from her face with an impatient gesture, and Chad remembered how that silky mass had felt under his searching fingers. Although she was fiercely angry, her distress in this situation was obvious. He softened for a moment.

"Look, I realize that it's short notice. But I read your lease and—"

"The hell with my lease." Tucker cut him off with a voice sharp with anger and frustration, directed squarely at him. "If what you want is more money, then let's negotiate."

"If I wanted to raise the rent, I would have said so. I don't. I'm selling the place. You need to be out by the end of the month."

"Don't you dare order me around like a child! I am not going to give in without a fight. I've worked too hard and too long to be knocked down to fulfill some grudge you've dreamed up against your father.''

Her words hit him like a slap across the face. ''Leave my father out of this. You've said more than enough about him already.''

''If your father were still alive, we wouldn't be having this conversation. Joshua Carver was a good man. He helped people. He was a man of integrity.'' Tucker snatched the note from his hand and tore it into small pieces. She flung them in the air and the bits of paper fluttered over them and rained to the floor. ''It's quite obvious that you are nothing like your father at all.''

Tucker turned and started out the front door. There was no point in talking further. She was even angrier than when she had arrived, and she wanted to get outside and away from Chad Carver, as far away as possible. She needed time to think, time to formulate a plan.

Chad caught up with her as she reached the second of the three steps back to the street. He grabbed her arm roughly, stopping her short. His fingers pressed into the flesh of her upper arm, startling her with his strength. The force of his grip lifted her close to him.

''You can think whatever you like about me. I don't much care.'' Chad's face was barely three inches from her own, and she felt the spicy warmth of his breath on her skin. His voice was low now, and evenly modulated, as though he was telling her something he wanted to be absolutely certain she understood. ''But I'm going to tell you the truth about my father. I'm going to make you understand.'' His eyes were wild, an angry sea of blue and green, seething with a range of dark emotions that frightened her. What was happening inside this man? She pulled back involuntarily, but was held fast by the iron grip on her arm.

Suddenly, Chad looked at his hand on her arm as if seeing it for the first time, almost as if it were someone else's hand holding fast to Tucker. He instantly released his hold, as if he'd been burned, and stepped back. She touched the place where his hand had been.

''I'm sorry. I didn't mean to hurt you.'' Chad's shoulders sagged, and he suddenly seemed much older. ''I thought you should know the truth; but it's too late for that now. You don't care what the truth is. It has nothing to do with you. I'm very sorry this happened.'' He turned and walked slowly back into the house.

Tucker watched his broad back disappear through the open doorway. She was free to leave, but suddenly she didn't want to. Something in his resigned tone moved her. The hot anger that had brought her here was banked for the moment, overshadowed by the desire to know what was behind Chad Carver. Something had been stirred up inside her when she met him, a feeling of shared pain, an echo of understanding. She didn't want to leave without finding its source.

She stepped silently into the entryway of the house. To the left was Joshua's office. Although she had only been there a handful of times in the last few years, Tucker recognized the huge old wooden desk and filing cabinets, and the dozens of old photos that hung on the walls in mismatched frames.

Chad was down on one knee by a group of cardboard boxes, labeling them with a black marker. His head was bent with concentration. He didn't look up as she entered the room. She waited, lingering near the door.

"I thought you were leaving." Chad's voice was even, but ragged and tinged with impatience. He did not look up from his work.

"You said you wanted me to understand. I've decided I want to know." The morning sun shafted at an angle through the air, creating dusty columns of light in the cluttered room.

"It doesn't matter." Chad barely glanced in her direction as he stacked two of the smaller boxes on top of the larger one. "I was wrong. There's no point in dredging up all that garbage now. It's a waste of time for both of us."

"I want to know." Tucker waited. Chad continued working. "Chad, please. Tell me about Joshua. Tell me about your father."

Chad straightened up, focusing on her for the first time since she entered the room. His eyes, that only a few moments earlier had been aflame with emotion, were guarded, almost cool. His voice was even, passionless. "All right. I'll tell you. And then you can leave."

His words stung her, and Tucker shifted awkwardly, uncertain, but Chad gestured toward the worn armchair facing the desk. She sat down. Chad sat behind the desk. The dark, pitted surface of the old desk stretched between them, littered with files, papers, and curling snapshots. Chad cleared the area in front of him with a sweep of his arm. He spread his hands out flat on the desktop. His hands were big and broad, with long, powerful fingers. His fingertips were square and calloused. A few light lines of faded scar tissue spidered over the knuckles of his right hand in sharp contrast to his tan.

Chad began suddenly, breaking the awkward silence. "My mother died two days before my ninth birthday." He studied the pitted top of the desk, his face an impassive mask. "I used to lie awake nights and ask God why He had taken her, why He couldn't have taken me instead." His eyes met hers. "Or my father."

Tucker felt the familiar sting of loss within her. "Your father never remarried?"

"No." Chad's lips twisted in a smile of irony.

"He always used to say, 'It's just you and me now, son. Two men on their own.' "

"He took care of you all by himself?"

"If you want to call it that. What he mostly did was look for sympathy in the bottom of a bottle. It wasn't too bad for the first few years. But I learned how to take care of myself early. After the first year or so, I was the one taking care of him."

"Are you saying he was an alcoholic?" Tucker tried to reconcile what she was hearing with the kindly old man she remembered.

Chad shrugged. "You can call it whatever you want to. At least he was predictable. And in the beginning, as long as he stuck to our little family routine, things weren't that bad. Most nights, I would make dinner for us. He would park himself in his favorite chair by the fire with a bottle of Old Granddad and a glass, and tell me everything he had done for me that day: how many passengers he'd taken out, how hard he had worked on the boat. All the crap he'd put up with. All because of me. Everything was because of me."

Chad's eyes darkened as he plunged more deeply into memory. "I felt guilty. Guilty for being a burden to my father. Guilty for making him have to work so hard. Guilty because my mother had died, and I secretly wished it had been him instead."

He paused, his fingers tracing an invisible pattern on the scarred surface of the desk. "We would eat, and he would finish the bottle, and by the time I finished the dishes he would pass out in his chair. I got pretty good at getting him upstairs and into bed."

"What a terrible life for a child." Tucker felt sick to her stomach.

"Actually, those were the easy times. Some nights he wouldn't come home for hours, and when he did, he didn't want to talk. He would just slam the front door so I'd know he was home, but he wouldn't say anything at all. That's when I knew I had better steer clear of him if I wanted to stay out of trouble. It was one of those quiet nights that he knocked out four of my teeth."

"My God." The sick feeling in her stomach grew worse.

Chad shrugged. "When that happened, I was twelve, and big for my age. I fought back." He smiled, a bitter expression that was devoid of any humor. "And that was the last time he laid a hand on me."

Tucker focused on one of the faded snapshots littering the desk. A family of three: a smiling young couple, arms locked around one another, and a sturdy little blond boy wedged between them, posing proudly in front of a new-looking building. She recognized it as her shop.

"Why didn't anyone try to help him, try to help you?"

"Most people didn't realize how bad it was. Some people suspected, I'm sure, but they figured it wasn't any of their business. Most people don't want to get between a father and his kid."

He picked up the photo that Tucker had been looking at and studied it silently for a moment. "Besides, my father never had a problem making people like him when he wanted to. He could really be the life of the party. But since the old man mostly liked to drink at home, and he didn't burn the house down, I think most folks probably thought there was no harm in him having a few."

Tucker felt outraged and angry and powerless, all at the same time. "Didn't you ever say anything to anyone? Tell someone who could help you, tell some other adult what was happening?"

"Are you kidding? I was so ashamed, I would do anything to keep people from knowing. When I was little, somehow it all felt like my fault. Everything that happened seemed connected to me. Later on, when I figured out that wasn't true, it was too late anyway."

Chad shifted in his chair, collecting memories. "By the time I was in high school, I had to take care of the business as well. The old man wasn't much good for anything by then, so he just let me do everything—take the passengers out, keep the boat in shape. Somewhere along the way, I just took it all on as my responsibility. Everything except deposit the money; somehow he always managed to show up sober enough to make it down to the bank.''

Chad leaned back in his chair, lacing his fingers behind his head. He didn't look at Tucker. His gaze was fastened at some imaginary point above her head, where his memories were unfolding for his review. ''I never understood how he did it, but he always seemed to know exactly how many passengers had been out that day, and how much money I'd brought in, even when he'd been gone all day. I tried to skim some of the money off the top a couple of times, but he always caught me.'' Chad laughed, a brief, humorless bark. ''For a drunk, he kept a hell of a set of books, I must admit.'' He jerked his thumb back toward the file cabinets he'd been in the process of clearing out.

''I was patient. I worked hard, I got good grades in school. I knew that one day I would get off this island and away from him. I got a partial scholarship to college, and the old man agreed to pay for the rest, as long as I came home to work during the summer.''

''So you went to college on the mainland.''

''Yes. UCLA. The old man pretty much shut down the business during the off-season, and I came home to run it every summer. That was our deal, our truce, and it almost worked out the whole time I was in school.''

''So what happened? What didn't work out?''

''My senior year I came home for spring break.

I wasn't supposed to come home that week; the old man had agreed to let me take a camping trip with my roommates. But the trip was cancelled, and I came home unexpectedly.''

Chad snorted in disgust. ''I figured it was for the best—that's a busy week for tourists here. He would need my help. I didn't tell him I was coming. I got to the shop about ten Saturday morning, but everything was locked; he hadn't even bothered to open up. I went to the house. The front door was ajar. I searched downstairs, but he wasn't there. Then I heard laughter from his bedroom upstairs. And that's where I found him.''

''Drunk?'' Tucker's voice matched the cool tone of Chad's narrative.

''Yes, and he wasn't alone. He was having quite the private party. He was in bed with this cocktail waitress from the Chi Chi Club. Darlene, one of his best drinking buddies. She was maybe twenty-two, twenty-three years old. Both of them naked and drunk out of their minds. They were still working on last night's party.''

Chad stood up and paced to the wall, as if to study one of the old photos there. Tucker waited silently, knowing he would continue when he was ready.

''I should have walked out. I should have turned around and walked out the door, but something just snapped inside of me. I lost control. I told him I was sick and tired of taking care of him all these years. I wasn't going to let him waste my life the way he had wasted his. He could drink the rest of his life away with his scummy friends if he wanted to, but this was the end of the line for me." Chad turned back toward her. "Then I nearly broke his jaw."

"You hit him?"

"No. But I wanted to. I really wanted to. Instead, I put my fist through the window. Got blood all over the bedroom. Quite a mess."

"My God!" The image sprung vividly into Tucker's mind, a younger version of Chad, angry, bloodied. It disturbed her deeply.

"It wasn't serious. The old man just laughed. He laughed and laughed. I bandaged up my hand and left the island that afternoon." Chad rubbed the scarred area over his knuckle in an unconscious gesture of memory. "I was back at school that night."

"Did you ever speak to him again?"

"Yes, a couple of months later. I called him the night before graduation. I guess I was feeling kind of sentimental."

"What did he say?"

"He told me to stay away. He said he didn't want me to come home. Not then, not ever. Which was fine with me. I never saw him again."

Chad rubbed the corner of his mouth with his thumb. "I traveled around quite a bit after that. I wrote to him now and then, usually a couple of times a year, told him where I was, what I was doing. I don't know why; I guess so he would know I was still alive. He never wrote back.''

Tucker wanted to say something, to offer some comfort, but she knew words would be inadequate. She knew all too well how little the condolences of well-meaning strangers were worth. Chad had told his story with little visible emotion, almost as if he were recounting something that had happened to someone else a long time ago. Yet she recognized the undercurrent of his pain, unexpressed in words, but very real and present. She waited silently for him to continue.

''All I care about now is getting through all this stuff,'' Chad gestured at the cluttered office. ''I want to sell the house, the shop, get the estate settled.'' Chad met her eyes for the first time in several minutes. ''And when that's all done, I will never have to come back here again, or spend another minute thinking about that old bastard.'' He returned to packing the half-full box of books in the corner of the room without looking back at her..

Silence filled the room like a palpable presence. Tucker felt as if he had forgotten she was there in the room with him. She dropped her eyes to the piles of photographs littering the desktop. She picked up the stack with the smiling family on top, slowly flipping through the rest of the photos.

She recognized Chad in a number of them, growing up through his childhood to young manhood. In some of them, he was carefree and happy. But most of them captured the deep quality of secret sadness; a sense that not all was as it appeared to be.

At the bottom of the stack were what appeared to be more recent photos, most in color. Tucker flipped quickly through a series of school pictures of Chad, hesitating on one, uncertain what it was about that picture that made her stop. A moment later, the realization hit her.

The child in the photo wasn't Chad. She glanced back at the family picture by the boat shop, then returned to the one that had caught her attention. This series of pictures was recent, and the boy certainly bore a striking resemblance to Chad, but he was definitely not him. Chad's childhood pictures showed a younger version of his strong, masculine features; this boy's face, although similar in shape and coloring, was much more delicately made.

Tucker turned the photo over. In an unfamiliar hand was written "Jamie, Age Five." Who was this little boy? She looked up to find Chad watching her from across the room.

"What's so interesting?" He was watching her through eyes half closed in suspicion.

"Who's Jamie?"

"Who?" Chad looked confused. "I don't know who you're talking about."

Tucker offered one of the photos from the stack. Chad took it and studied the snapshot for a full minute before he spoke. For the moment, his face was expressionless.

"I've never seen this kid before in my life." Chad quickly leaned over Tucker's shoulder. He impatiently sifted through the photos on the desk, tossing aside the snapshots of himself and his father as he searched. In a few moments, he had separated out nearly a dozen pictures of this unknown child, from infancy to about nine. They were both silent as he examined the series of photos.

"It was true." Chad's voice was so quiet she wasn't sure for a moment he had spoken aloud.

"That rumor you heard about me; I mean at least part of it was true. The girl that I supposedly got pregnant and deserted. The one that left the island before she had the baby. That must have been Darlene they were talking about. She really must have been pregnant."

Chad shuffled through the photos again, this time checking the backs for dates, finding a few, making some mental calculations before he spoke again.

"And this must be her child."

"But you said it wasn't true. You said it was all a lie." Tucker studied Chad's face as he examined the photos. What was he saying? She couldn't keep from asking the question that was uppermost in her mind.

"Are you telling me this little boy is your son?"

"No. He is not my son." Chad's voice was still quiet, but now shook slightly with the depth of whatever emotions he was experiencing. "But I think he may be my brother."

EIGHT

Realization burst upon Tucker like the uncomfortable glare of a bare light bulb switched on in a dark room. Darlene was indeed pregnant when she left Catalina ten years ago, but not with Chad's child. She had been carrying Joshua's baby. And judging from the number of photos and the age of the boy in them, Darlene hadn't disappeared, but had kept in regular contact with Joshua over the years.

Yet no one else had known the truth. Joshua had hidden his own involvement with Darlene, and let his friends and neighbors believe that Chad had run away from his responsibilities, while he played the part of the neglected father. That must have been why he had told Chad never to return home. His deceit would have become obvious.

Chad's face was ash gray beneath his tan. He slowly sat down behind his father's old desk, easing himself into the worn leather chair. The series of photos of Jamie were lined up in two rows. As he studied them silently, Tucker looked back and forth between the man opposite her and the pictures of the boy on the desk in front of him. So alike in appearance, close in blood, and yet until now, unknown to one another. She was suddenly uncomfortable, as if she were intruding into a private moment where she neither belonged nor was welcome. She cleared her throat, searching for words.

"I don't know what to say. This must be an incredible shock to you."

Chad didn't answer, but kept looking at the rows of photos, lost in thought. He moved one of the pictures a fraction of an inch, bringing it into perfect alignment with the others. Tucker waited a moment longer, then stood up. "Chad, I think I had better go."

Chad looked up, and in his eyes she saw raw need. Gone was the cool demeanor he had maintained while telling her of his childhood. Here was a man whose emotions were running very near the surface. Tucker was brought back to those moments at Starlight Beach; this was that same man. The man who had kissed her, and whose kiss she had

returned with a rush of feeling that she hadn't
known in years.

"Please stay." His eyes underscored the words.

The simplicity of his request moved her more
than if he'd pleaded with her. "Okay, if you want
me to, I will." Unspoken gratitude was written in
his face.

Chad ran his hand through his hair, an unconscious gesture that was becoming familiar to her.
He looked out the window at the bright morning.
Tucker followed his line of vision. A small boy
on a bicycle rode past the house, a scruffy brown
dog following close behind. The boy leaned back
and joyfully shouted some command to the dog,
who barked sharply in response.

"Let's get some air in here." Chad opened the
two windows facing the street, pushing them up
as wide as they could go, and pulling back the
faded yellow curtains. He stood for a moment,
looking out at the narrow street, lined with tall
eucalyptus trees.

Tucker waited, wondering what was running
through Chad's mind. He broke from his reverie.
When he spoke, his voice was decisive. "I want
to know more about all this. If she sent him all
these pictures, it means they were communicating
with each other, and often. Who knows what else
we might find in all this junk?"

Tucker nodded silently as Chad pulled open one

of the file cabinet drawers. What did he think he was going to find?

"You take this one," he said gesturing her toward it, "and I'll start with the desk." Chad sat down behind the desk and opened one of the drawers. He pulled out a thick stack of manilla files.

"What exactly are we looking for?" Tucker peered into the file cabinet.

"I don't know. Anything to do with Jamie. I want to know where he is. If he's my brother, I want to find him." His eyes burned with a new intensity, not the anger and hurt she had seen before, but a sense of yearning. "It's like I'm looking for a piece of myself. I want to find out the truth; about him and about my father and Darlene. I'm tired of all the lies. I think it's time."

Tucker's heart was pounding as she began to investigate the contents of the file cabinet's drawer. She didn't know exactly why, but she felt there was a mystery for her to discover here as well.

At the bottom of the drawer were yellowed magazines, calendars, and stacks of old pamphlets advertising the glass bottom boat. Joshua apparently was something of a pack rat; it looked as if he'd saved everything that had ever passed through his life. She stacked some of the dusty magazines beside the cabinet.

She glanced at Chad behind the desk. He was leafing through a notebook of green paper, filled with Joshua's spidery black handwriting. Every few pages he would stop and run a finger down the page, reading entries. A few seconds later, he closed the notebook and tossed it aside. He pulled some more stacks of paper from the desk drawer.

Tucker didn't find anything of interest in the first drawer, so she closed it and moved on to the bottom drawer. This one seemed to be mostly old bank records: boxes and boxes of cancelled checks, deposit books, and bank statements. Nothing promising. She was about to move on, when an idea formed in her mind.

Tucker opened the first box of canceled checks. The dates scrawled on the end of the box were more than five years ago, not long after she had moved to Catalina. She recognized almost all the payees that the checks were made out to: the local grocery store, the pharmacy, Dr. Stevens, the telephone company. Not too different from her own check register. She flipped quickly through the stack, searching for something else. She found what she was looking for near the bottom of the box.

Pay to the Order of Darlene Wilton. $1000.00 The date on the check was June 1; it was the first check Joshua had written that month.

Tucker put that box aside, and searched for the previous one in the sequence. A few seconds later, she found what her hunch had told her she would: another check, same amount, made out to Darlene. Again it was the very first check of the month.

She worked backwards, leafing through more than two years' worth of canceled checks, pulling out the ones she wanted before she stopped. Every month, it was there.

"Chad, I've found something you should see." She laid the checks out in sequence on the desk in front of him. "It was the first check Joshua wrote every month."

Chad traced his father's signature on the nearest one with a finger. "Every month. Like clockwork."

"Do you want me to keep going back?" Tucker checked the contents of the file drawer. "There are a couple more years' worth here, and if he saved these, the others must be here somewhere."

"No, I don't need to see any more. I think it's pretty clear." Chad's eyes met hers, and Tucker was struck by the conflicting emotions that struggled there. "Tucker, obviously he must have cared about her, and Jamie, too. Why didn't they stay together? Why did he lie about what happened?"

"I don't know, Chad."

Chad sighed wearily. He stood up and looked out the window again. "You know what I have to do now, don't you?"

Tucker's throat hurt when she spoke, like it was closing on her words. "I think so."

"I've got to contact Darlene." Chad was looking out into the quiet street, but he didn't seem to be seeing the scene outside. "She must not know that he's dead. I don't think anyone but my father knew about her and Jamie. No one will have called her."

Tucker nodded silently, anticipating his next words.

"I have to do it. I've got to sell everything. Darlene will need the money to take care of Jamie. My father did the right thing for once in his sorry life. Now I've got to finish it for him." Chad turned toward her, and took her hand gently. "I'm sorry, Tucker. It has to be done."

"I know." Tucker brushed the back of her hand roughly over her stinging eyes. She would not let him see what was happening inside her right now. She banged her shin sharply against the chair leg as she stood up, and she was glad for the momentary distraction of the pain. "You just do what you have to do, and I'll do what I have to do."

Tucker was at the front door before Chad could find his voice. She opened the door and stepped outside, and the bright morning sun glared painfully in her eyes. She squinted against the brightness.

"Tucker, wait a second, I want to—"

She closed the door behind her firmly, cutting off Chad's words. There wasn't any point in prolonging this scene. As much as it hurt to think about, she knew that Chad was trying to do the right thing. She was simply caught in the middle of circumstances. It really had nothing to do with her at all. She needed to remember that and get working on a solution for her situation.

Tucker walked the short distance back to her shop at a fast clip, struggling to keep her mind focused on the problem of the shop. Where could she move? How much more could she afford to pay? What was she going to do? The overwhelming fact that would not go away was that she would have to do something. She had no choice. She was on her own. She was alone. The Ice Goddess of Avalon.

As she walked, she was aware of another fact, another realization, that was growing in her mind, one that she wanted to avoid even more than the financial ones she now faced.

When this was over—when the shop was sold and she had relocated who knew where—something else would be over, too. Something that hadn't really even started, but without even being aware, she had let herself begin to hope for. Something that for a brief moment had moved her in a way she had thought was gone for her forever.

But hope didn't change reality. The fact remained, unchanged. When this was over, Chad Carver would be leaving Catalina for good.

NINE

It had been a quiet day. Tucker had a few customers, but there was no question that the season was over. She spent most of her time catching up on cleaning the equipment that had come back at the end of the three-day weekend, and making some minor repairs. She moved the units that were scheduled for their periodic overhaul into the shop. She would get them done gradually over the next few months.

Usually, this was a day she looked forward to all summer long, the beginning of the annual slowdown, when the island once again became the quiet haven that had drawn her here six years ago. Catalina in the fall and winter months was like a private retreat that more than made up for the hectic tourist months.

But this year, the first day of the off-season was not a happy day. Tucker was preoccupied with concerns for the future. She knew she had to start taking action, but she felt overwhelmed by the prospect of beginning.

Tucker finished sweeping the shop floor and looked at the clock. It was 5:30. She might as well knock off on time tonight. Even though it had been slow today, she was tired. Maybe tomorrow she would have the energy to begin looking for a place to relocate. She put the wide push broom in its place in the corner, and pulled the double doors closed for the day. They seemed heavier than usual.

As she fumbled with the keys at the front door, she heard the gate to the yard click shut. When she turned around, Chad was leaning back against the gate.

"Hi." His smile was thin and strained. "I'm probably the last person you wanted to see tonight."

"No, not the last person." Tucker tucked her keys into her shoulder bag. "Maybe the next-to-last." She remembered the first time they had stood together here. Was that really only a few days ago? Chad looked older to her now, more careworn.

"Listen, I know this is a lot to ask, but would you take a walk with me? I really need to talk to you." His words were low and even, but carried a quiet intensity that she felt deep in her body.

"Okay. I guess I have to walk home anyway."

He smiled, but this time with a touch of the warmth she remembered from that first day. "We'll take the long way."

Tucker locked the gate behind them. The sun was still high in the sky, and was turning the waters of the harbor into a glistening mirror. They started walking in the direction of the Cabrillo mole, where the large commercial boat that crossed the channel every day docked. They passed the closed ticket booths, the empty turnstiles and vacant dock.

"Another season's over." Tucker waited for a reply, but Chad nodded and said nothing. *I thought you wanted to talk,* she mused to herself. They continued along Pebbly Beach Road as it rounded Lovers' Cove. The small rocky beach was empty. Chad stopped, looking out over the water. A fish splashed somewhere out in the cove.

"Darlene's dead." Chad kept his eyes trained out over the water, as if he were watching something.

Tucker felt a strange flash of emotion, shock and regret together. An odd way to feel for someone she had never met. "When? What happened?"

"A little more than two years ago. Car accident, on the freeway out of L.A. Jamie's been in foster homes ever since it happened." Chad's voice was thick with an emotion that Tucker couldn't pin down.

"How did you find out?"

"The old man had old newspaper clippings about the accident. She was drunk at the time. That's what the newspaper said anyway."

"What about the boy? Was he hurt?"

"He wasn't in the car." Relief flooded through her. Chad was still looking out over the water when he spoke again. "Tucker?"

"Yes?"

Chad turned toward her and looked directly into her eyes. She had never seen a man in the grip of such powerful and contradictory emotions. She had a strong sense that Chad's vision of the world was changing; that he suddenly no longer knew what to expect. It was a feeling she remembered well from those first months after she had lost Peter.

"There's more. I found a file on Jamie. Lots of legal mumbo-jumbo, but the upshot of the whole thing is—" Chad's voice was rough with feelings he was holding back. He cleared his throat several times, and shoved his hands roughly into the pockets of his jeans. Tucker waited, saying nothing, letting him work it through for himself.

"Apparently soon after Darlene died, Joshua tried to get custody of Jamie. The court denied it, but he kept fighting for it, nearly two years. He had to jump through a lot of hoops, but the custody issue was finally settled. However, it didn't matter. It was too late.''

"What do you mean?''

Chad cleared his throat again, but his voice was still not under his complete control. "The court granted him custody, but he never knew about it. I found the letter in that big stack of unopened mail that's arrived here in the last two months. Judging from the postmark, it probably got here about two weeks after he died.''

The silence that fell between them was thick with unspoken feeling. They watched the water in front of them, now stirring gently with an evening breeze. The sun was setting behind the island now, and the waters of the little cove were rapidly darkening. Once the sun was behind the mountain, it would soon be night. Tucker reached out to touch Chad's arm lightly, a wordless gesture of support and understanding. He touched her hand in response.

"It's getting dark. I'll walk you home.''

"Okay.'' They started walking toward town. Tucker searched for something to say, but words didn't come. Chad was a large, silent presence beside her in the dusk. What was going through his mind right now?

The ground beneath their feet was uneven, and Tucker stumbled slightly in the darkness. Chad's hands were there immediately, steadying her.

"Thanks.'' She let his arm stay around her

waist as they walked on. They walked the rest of the way back to Tucker's house in silence.

Night had fallen when they stopped on the sidewalk in front of the house. Tucker felt Chad's reluctance to leave her, and she found she didn't want him to leave her alone yet either.

"Do you want to sit outside for a while? There's a nice view of the stars from my porch."

"That would be great."

They settled on the wooden porch swing. The night was growing cooler, and a few of the night birds were chirping softly. The porch swing creaked softly as they rocked back and forth. Tucker felt that Chad was holding something back, something else that he was struggling with, but she didn't want to pry. She knew that waiting was sometimes the best thing. She didn't have to wait long.

"Tucker."

"Yes?"

"He's going to be here tomorrow."

"Who?"

"Jamie."

"Chad, what are you talking about?"

"He's arriving by plane tomorrow. It was set up more than six months ago. He thinks he's coming to live with Joshua—with his father." Chad rubbed his eyes, as if to see better in the darkness. "As far as the child welfare people know, Joshua will be there to pick him up in the morning. And that's what Jamie thinks, too.''

"My God, Chad, what are you going to do?" Tucker's heart ached with concern for a little boy she had never met.

Chad's eyes burned in the night. "I don't know. I honestly don't know." Chad stood and walked to the low rail that bordered the porch. He leaned back against the rail, his face lit by a shaft of light from the newly risen moon. "I don't know what I think anymore. Everything's changing. Damn it, I thought that once the old man was dead, everything would be simple. It's not."

"Chad, life is never simple, even when it should be, believe me."

"Joshua wasn't much of a father. I don't know why he would be so willing to try it again." Chad snorted shortly. "I'm pretty sure the day I left was one of the happiest days of his life."

"Chad, I don't really think that's true. Your father had some problems, some very serious problems, that's clear from what you've said about how he acted when you were growing up. You're angry at him, and I don't blame you. But I don't think you really know everything about him. Maybe the reason he wanted to get custody of Jamie was to try to get back some of what he lost with you."

"I don't know about that. All I know is that he was a rotten father to me." Chad sat back down beside her, defeated. The swing moved with the force of his large frame. "And hell, I can't say for sure I'd be any better. Tucker, I don't even know what to say to a ten-year-old boy. He's going to get off that plane tomorrow morning, and I don't even know the first thing to say."

"I guess you can start with 'Hello.' "

"I'll have to tell him about Joshua. And then I'm going to have to contact the authorities. There's nothing I can do for him. He'll just have to go back to wherever he came from." Chad's shoulders sagged with weariness. The day's events had taken their toll on him. "Will it ever be over?"

"What, Chad? Will what ever be over?"

Chad rubbed the back of his neck, as if searching for the source of some lingering pain, and laughed bitterly. "This mess. This big mess that seems to keep following me around. It seems like I've been trying to make sense out of it since I was nine years old."

Tucker's heart wrenched within her. She put her hand at the back of his neck where his own had been a moment earlier and felt the knots of tension there. She wondered how long he had carried them there. She gently kneaded them for a moment.

"Chad, some bad things have happened to you. There's no question about it. But you can't stay angry forever. Believe me, I was angry for a very long time."

Chad raised his head. He studied her face for a long minute before speaking. "What were you angry about?"

"It was a long time ago, Chad." *But sometimes it seems like yesterday,* she thought.

He captured her hand between his two. His hands were warm and solid. "Please tell me."

Tucker considered, but only for a moment. She wanted to tell him. It would hurt, she knew that, but it was the right thing to do. "Before I came to Catalina, I was married to a man I met in college. He was a wonderful man. I loved him very much." Chad tightened his hold on her hand. "I had plans for every day for years to come; we would do everything two people had ever dreamed of, and we would be together always. But that's not what life had in store for us."

"What happened?"

"Peter was in law school, and we were living in downtown L.A. It was not a great neighborhood, but it was the best we could afford, and besides, we were young. We didn't worry about those kinds of things then." The words never got any easier to say, but Tucker wanted Chad to hear them.

"We had one car between us, so Peter usually took the bus back and forth from school. The bus let him off three blocks from our apartment. One night, he was coming home late after a night class and three men followed him off the bus when he got off. They jumped him for his wallet. He should have just given it to them, but, like a fool, Peter fought back.'' Tucker closed her eyes, just for an instant, then opened them. She took a deep breath before continuing. ''They beat him, very badly. I guess they were angry that he had dared to fight back. They really hurt him.''

''Tucker,'' Chad spoke very softly now, ''I am so sorry. You don't have to tell me any more.''

''No; but I want you to understand. Someone called the police, but, of course, the men were gone by the time they arrived. The paramedics took him to the hospital, and by the time I got there, he was unconscious. He died early the next day. It was a brain embolism, probably from a kick to the head the doctor said.''

Chad started to put his arms around Tucker, as if to comfort her, but she stopped him, putting her hands flat against his chest, leaning into him and speaking very clearly.

''Chad, I was angry. Angry at those men; men who were never caught, who were never punished. Angry at the city. Angry at myself, angry at Peter, angry at the world. I was even angry at God. How could He let something like this happen?'' Tucker took a deep breath before she continued.

''And that anger drove me to do something. My old life was gone, gone with Peter, but I had to keep living. I couldn't change the past, but I could do something about my future. I came back to

Catalina, for good this time. This island had been a special place to the two of us, and I just couldn't live in the city anymore." She paused, ordering the memories that flooded her mind.

"I used the little bit of money from Peter's life insurance to set up my business. And believe me, Chad, I was still very bitter and very angry. And the anger kept the hurt so fresh inside me that sometimes I thought I couldn't stand to live another day."

She paused, remembering a day that she'd never spoken of to anyone, a day so dark she had come close to ending her misery with the whole bottle of sleeping pills the doctors had given her. Only fear that she didn't have enough for a fatal dose had stopped her. She shook that memory off, squeezing Chad's hands tightly.

"So I had to let it go. I had to give up being angry at life for taking Peter from me. I had to forgive the world for being a place where bad things can happen. And do you know what happened? I got better. Slowly, I got better, day by day. I still miss Peter very, very much. I always will. But that's the past. And I'm not going to let the bad parts of the past destroy the good parts of today."

Chad brushed a few strands of Tucker's hair back from her face. Her gray eyes shone with the intensity and emotion that had captivated him the first moment he'd seen her, that moment at the shop that he would always remember, he in the darkness and she in the light. Suddenly, he could identify what it was in those eyes that had captured him that first night; it was courage, and suffering, and peace. A hard-won peace, one that had been bought with a bitter price.

He longed for that peace. The years since he had left home had been filled with wandering, with odd jobs in strange places. Beautiful places, but not home, none of them home. He had told himself that it was wanderlust that kept him moving on, that he liked the rootless life. He had told himself that his time with the women he had met in those strange places had been honest, because he always told them up front that one day he would leave them. That had been okay with most of them.

But looking into Tucker's eyes told him he had been wrong. It wasn't wanderlust that had kept him moving on, it was a search, a search for that peace. It was a solitary search, a secret search, one that he had let no other man or woman share with him.

He had held people at a distance, so that he wouldn't have to see his own pain and loneliness reflected back in their eyes. It was better that no one know him, that no one come close enough to feel the anger and disappointment that still controlled him no matter how much he might deny it to himself.

Tucker Ryan was different. She recognized what he was about. That was what had both intrigued him and unnerved him from the first moments they had been together. She could have been wrapped up in herself, holding within her only her own very private suffering, with no room for anyone else's troubles. But she wasn't. She recognized his pain and rage. She saw him for what he was, but she was still here with him now. She was still here.

"Chad?" Tucker leaned forward, trying to see his face more clearly in the dim light of the evening. What was going through his mind right now? "Does it make any sense? Does anything I've told you make any sense to you at all?"

He didn't speak for a long minute. His eyes were dark, nearly the color of the ocean at night. Chad reached out and caught her chin in one hand and held it. The warmth of him felt good against her cool skin.

"Tucker P. Ryan, you are an amazing woman." He bent his head gently down, and guided her face to his lips. He pressed his lips tenderly on her forehead, letting them linger for a long moment. His other arm gently cradled her around her shoulders.

"Thank you." His lips whispered gently against her forehead, a fluttering caress of words. "Thank you for being who you are." He pulled her cheek against his chest, and the heat of his body warmed

her through the fabric of his sweatshirt. She
thought she could almost hear the beating of his
heart within his chest.

They stayed in that position, not moving. The
only sound Tucker heard was their own slow
breathing, and far in the distance, the ocean. It
had been hard to talk about Peter tonight, as it
always was, but somehow it had seemed so right,
so important. And now, now that the words had
been said, she felt different than she usually did
after revisiting those painful times.

Instead of the familiar pain that reliving those
memories always brought to her, she felt a sense
of completeness. Usually she retained her serenity
by letting those parts of her past remain stored
away, in that area of the mind where distant memories are locked away, hidden from daily review,
though never truly forgotten. In the past, repeating
the events surrounding Peter's death had disrupted
her peace, destroyed her serenity, and left her
under a black cloud of depression that sometimes
took a week to clear.

This time though, as she repeated the story to
Chad, different feelings had come forward. The
pain had been there, of course, and the sense of
loss and some of the anger, too. But only briefly;
when the telling was done, they had slipped away
with the words. In their place was a sense of clo-
sure that was new to Tucker, a sense of perspective. Somehow, in trying to tell Chad about the

forgiveness he needed, her own had come back to her in a fuller, more complete way as well. Something was changing inside her, and that something had to do with helping Chad find some answers to his own past.

The warmth of Chad's body felt good against her skin. He smelled like a mixture of simple soap and the ocean air. It was a good, comforting smell. She felt so peaceful and safe, she was near dozing off. Beneath the thin fleece of his sweatshirt, she felt the muscles of his chest shift slightly, and he gently pulled her by the shoulders to a sitting position. His face was only inches from hers, and his eyes were looking at her with a searching need.

"You have beautiful eyes." The words rumbled out from somewhere deep within him, and carried emotion that went beyond the words. He gently took her face between his hands. She felt tremendous strength in the big hands that now held her so tenderly. Carefully he smoothed the skin at the corner of her mouth with the broad pad of one thumb, like he might caress the delicate petal of a rose. The sensation of his work-roughened hands against her face was a delicious contrast of textures, hard and soft, rough and smooth, tough and gentle meeting in first tentative explorations.

His eyes studied her as if he were memorizing her features, searing them upon his mind forever. His lips were parted with breath, and she noticed how full and well formed they were. Tucker knew with sudden certainty that she wanted those lips on her own, that mouth searching hers.

He must have read the message in her eyes, for Chad bent his head and brought her lips to meet his in a gesture that was gentle, but filled with strength and urgency. His lips crushed firmly on her mouth, and the pressure was wonderfully right, perfectly matched to the desire that was growing within her. Chad tilted his head and his mouth gently began to work against her lips, needing more, demanding more of her. She let the gentle caresses of his mouth continue as long as she could bear it, then parted her lips to invite him in.

His mouth was warm, and tasted of the same earthy masculine essence she remembered so well from the day at Starlight Beach. He explored her mouth slowly, deliberately pleasuring secret places she didn't know she had. She responded in kind, tentative at first, then more confidently when she felt her tongue meeting the solid smoothness of his teeth and then the heat of his searching tongue.

Chad's hands were in her hair now, his long fingers tangling in the silky mass. Tucker's searching hands sought his shoulders and back, broad planes of solid muscle under her fingers. Her hands roamed, delighting in the feel of his hardness under her palms. The intensity of his kisses increased, fired by his pleasure at her touch. She caressed him more deliberately in response, and

Chad drew her closer to him with a single strong motion, crushing her breasts against his solid chest. His mouth claimed hers even more completely now with deep, probing strokes.

A powerful shudder passed through Chad that Tucker felt through her whole body. Chad pulled back, slowly breaking their kiss, and sitting up straight, but his hands still held possessively to her shoulders. Tucker released her hold on his back, and her hands dropped onto his thighs. Through the worn denim of his jeans, she felt the steely cords of muscle sharply contract under her hands in instant response to her touch. She didn't remove her hands.

He took a deep breath, and looked straight into her face, and Tucker could see the beating of his heart in the column of his neck, a strong fast pulse of desire. "Tucker, we've got to stop. I don't want to stop, believe me." He licked his lower lip, as if to taste the flavor of her mouth that might linger there. "But if I don't stop now, I might not be able to, and then I'm afraid we'd be giving your neighbors quite a show." He looked as if he might kiss her again, but instead he smiled, a look full of need and desire, but controlled, considerate of her feelings. "I hope I didn't overwhelm you."

"You did." Tucker smiled, a little bashful. "But I liked it. I liked it very much." Her hands were growing warmer from the heat of Chad's thighs beneath them. Tucker grew serious, and when she spoke it was very slowly and deliberately. "I think we should go inside."

Chad looked at her for a long moment, trying to be sure of her meaning. His eyes were dark pools of longing. "Are you sure that's what you want?" His voice was an aching rumble of passion.

Tucker took a deep breath. Her world was changing, spinning around her in a crazy blur of feelings and sensations. She was conscious of the movement of the muscles of Chad's thighs beneath the palm of her hands, the scent of his body, the taste of his mouth. Things were happening inside her, a forceful whirlwind of thoughts and images that all swirled her into the shadowed depths of Chad's eyes.

But it all felt right; so very right. When she spoke, she was surprised by how calm her voice sounded.

"Yes, Chad. It's time."

TEN

Chad shut the door behind him and leaned against it, hands tucked behind his back, waiting. Tucker turned on a single lamp on a low table by a rocking chair, illuminating the tiny living room with a gentle, golden glow. The room was small and furnished simply with only a few pieces of furniture, but everything was perfectly to scale, creating a cozy world that seemed to have been created just for the two of them. In that moment, Chad realized that this was a home, a home in the sense that he had not known for many years.

Tucker crossed to him slowly, moving gracefully across the room. God, she was beautiful. Her hair was a tangled mass from his searching fingers, and her lips were swollen and moist from his mouth. Her eyes, gray and luminous, still glowed with that same magic that had drawn him to her, that had slowly and inexorably brought him to this moment.

She stopped right in front of him, as if she were waiting, but before he could move, to his great surprise and delight she reached for him. She put her arms around his neck and drew herself up to his lips, her mouth sweet and hot and willing. Chad groaned in response, and pulled her in tight to his body, leaning back against the door to support the two of them. Her full breasts, restrained by the light cotton blouse, pressed against his chest, and the pressure brought a responsive tightening in his loins.

Chad reached to cup one breast in his hand. Tucker moaned and leaned into him, filling his hand with warmth. Through the thin layers of cotton, his fingers found the hardening peak of her nipple. She moaned her pleasure into his mouth, and his fingers gently increased the pressure on the sensitive mound. Tucker raked her fingers down his chest, and his whole body trembled with a wave of pleasure.

Tucker slid her hands underneath Chad's sweatshirt, gasping at the heat of his bare skin. Her fingers examined with delight the planes of his body, entangling her fingers in the thatch of curls over the breadth of his chest, tracing by feel the path they made down to his flat abdomen, and then disappeared into the waistband of his jeans. All this she found blindly, letting her fingers remember the image of his body, the image that had stayed with her ever since she had seen him nearly naked the day of the dive. Chad groaned as her fingers traveled lower, down his lower abdomen, daring to dip an inch into the snug waist of his jeans where she knew the blond trail would fan out again. She let her fingers dip a fraction lower still, following the golden path.

"Tucker," he said, his voice low and guttural. His hands dropped to her hips, and pulled her pelvis tight against him. She felt the full length of his arousal against her belly. "I want you so much." He kissed her on the mouth, hard and deep.

Tucker pressed against him, her own desire growing stronger and stronger, fanned by feeling the strength of his need for her so firm against her body. He had touched her like a match to dry grass; the flash fire was sudden and hot, and unstoppable. Tucker pulled away and took his hand to lead him back to her bedroom.

Chad was surprised by Tucker's bedroom. The four-poster bed was covered with a quilt in a pattern of abundant yellow daisies, and the curtains at the windows were made of yards and yards of antique lace, tied back with wide grosgrain ribbons. Fresh daisies made a casual bouquet in a hand-painted pitcher on the antique dresser. Everything about the room was very feminine, not frilly or fussy, but each accessory showed the careful hand of a woman who loved beautiful things.

Tucker turned on a low lamp, then turned to Chad who stood waiting by the door. She looked suddenly uncertain, overwhelmed by what was happening between them. Was she sorry she had let things get this far? Chad tried to ignore the pressure in his loins that was growing greater every moment. He wasn't going to let her do anything she wasn't ready for; he knew in a sudden burst of insight that she meant too much to him to let anything happen that she might later regret. No matter what, he wouldn't let her be hurt again.

"Tucker, if you don't want this . . ." His voice trailed off as she approached him, all traces of uncertainty erased from her face. She stopped a few feet from him, and in silent answer slowly unbuttoned her blouse, revealing a white lacy brassiere beneath the cotton. Chad's heart was pounding as she removed the blouse and dropped it to the floor. Her full curves were barely restrained by the wispy cotton, and the swell of her breasts rose and fell with her breath. She opened her arms in a wordless gesture of invitation.

He was in her arms in an instant, covering her mouth, her throat, her shoulders with a rain of kisses. He buried his face in the hollow of her neck and inhaled deeply, reveling in her sweet scent, light and fresh like the first breath of air after a rain. He took deep breaths, as if to take the very essence of her into him.

Chad gently touched both of her breasts through the thin fabric of her brassiere, feeling them warm and swell beneath his hands. A moment later he had released the clasp, freeing their fullness to him. He stopped to look at her with a sense of awe. Her breasts were firm and high, creamy white in contrast to her tan. Her nipples were large and dark rose in color, already tightening with excitement.

"You are so beautiful." Chad brushed the white gold of her hair back off her shoulders. She looked at him with eyes that mingled trust and desire. He wanted to make everything perfect for her tonight. He bent his head gently over one breast, drawing her nipple into his mouth, caressing it with his lips and tongue into a hard peak of pleasure. Tucker moaned softly, and put her hand at the back of his head, pressing his mouth tighter against her.

Tucker let her head roll back as Chad moved to the other breast, to tease the other into the same tight rosebud of sensation. Her breathing became ragged as he worked his magic with his tongue, while still keeping the first one aroused with his gently probing fingers. The pleasure was almost unbearable as he cupped her with his hands. Finally, she needed more, more of him. She needed to feel him against her.

She gently drew his mouth from her breast, hushing his questioning lips with a kiss. She reached for the ribbing at the bottom of his sweatshirt and drew it over his head. Chad bent over to help her pull it off the final few inches, then she tossed it aside. She reveled for a moment at seeing his torso exposed, tracing the sculptured lines hungrily with her hands, this time seeing them with her eyes as well as her fingertips.

She found the flat dark circles of his nipples buried in the thatch of blond curls, and standing on tiptoe to reach, teased them into taut knots with her fingers and her mouth. He moaned, and drew her close to him, her breasts pressed against his chest, finally skin to skin, his hair-roughened body a delicious contrast to her smoothness. They stood like that for several long minutes, without speaking, hearing only the sound of their mingled breathing in the dimly lit room.

Tucker felt as if she stood at the edge of a strange ocean, ready to plunge into its unfamiliar waters. What would she discover? What dangers or delights would it hold for her? She did not know what she would find, but she believed that now, after six years of waiting on the shore, she was finally ready to take the plunge into the mysterious dark waters again.

Chad scooped her up and carried Tucker to her bed. He gently laid her down in the middle of the field of quilted flowers, and kissed her tenderly.

As he stood beside the bed, he carefully worked at the button at the top of her jeans, fingers trembling slightly, then slowly pulled down the zipper. She raised her hips to help him draw off her jeans, leaving her only in a wisp of white cotton panties. He quickly drew those off and tossed them aside.

Chad stopped and admired her, slowly letting his gaze slip down the length of her naked body, taking in each part of her, and then finally all of her. "Beautiful," he whispered, speaking only to himself, almost like a prayer. She felt a flush starting at her face warm her body down to her toes. Chad's honest appreciation of her body pleased her, and she didn't feel the self-consciousness she would have expected. It was as if she and Chad had already shared such emotional intimacies that this was the natural fulfillment of those exchanges, a completion of what had gone before.

Chad started to turn out the lamp that bathed the room in a soft light, but Tucker stopped him. "No. I want to see all of you."

Chad colored slightly, but seemed pleased. "Okay." He looked straight into her eyes as he shucked off his jeans and briefs. He stood still for a moment, waiting, his skin glowing golden in the low light.

Tucker sucked in her breath. He was like some magnificent wild animal. The sight of him stirred something deep and primal within her; it was a feeling she had never known before, but it came from a secret hidden place within her and it truly belonged to her alone.

He was a splendid sight, six feet two inches of lean muscle moving beneath skin the color of burnished bronze. His long legs were powerful, long, lean columns of strength. The blond curls across the breadth of his chest tapered down to a light spattering across his flat belly, becoming a coarse thatch surrounding his manhood, which betrayed the enormity of his need for her. She wanted him. She needed him with her now.

Tucker stretched out her arms to Chad, wordlessly calling him to her side. He was instantly beside her on the bed, his warm mouth reclaiming hers possessively. She felt the heat of him along the whole length of her body, her skin warming to his and returning the warmth to him.

Chad covered her face with kisses, his lips moving from her mouth to her cheeks to her throat, a series of quick, hot caresses that electrified her skin. His hands were moving over her body now, down to her hips. He caressed the length of her legs, the rough pads of his fingers drawing patterns of heat on her thighs, until his hand finally reached the downy blond mound. Tucker gasped when he touched her there, her body stiffening slightly, but she quickly relaxed, so light and caressing was his touch.

Their kisses became more urgent, more filled with mutual need as he gently dipped into her warm moisture, again and again, each time more deeply. Tucker moaned with pleasure, and reached down between them, longing to touch Chad, to hold the length of him in her hand. Her searching fingers closed around him, weighing the silken masculine heaviness of him in her hand, caressing him slowly.

Chad broke from her mouth, groaning with aching delight. "I can't wait any longer." His voice was husky with passion. "I want you, Tucker, now."

In answer, her fingers grasped him more firmly. "Yes. Yes, now." She was ready for him, ready as she had never been before in her life.

Chad swung himself over her, his strong arms suspending his broad torso over her, shielding her from the weight of his body. She guided him into her, a slow stroke that filled her as she gradually released herself, welcoming him in. They stayed still for a moment, savoring the first exquisite sensations of becoming one. Tucker brushed back the hair that had fallen over Chad's forehead, damp with sweat, and they kissed, their searching tongues the only part of them in motion.

Then Chad began their dance, agonizingly slow at first, then faster and faster, until they found the mutual rhythm they sought. Tucker gave herself over to the exquisite delight of union with an abandon she had never experienced before. They moved together, as if linked mentally as well as physically, each anticipating and meeting the other's movements in perfect synchronism.

Tucker was hungry to touch him, to experience every inch of him. Her hands roamed over his body, the solid surface of his back, the corded muscles of his thighs, and the tight round mounds of his buttocks, urging him on, as she rode closer and closer to fulfillment.

Her final pleasure broke over her like a succession of waves, one after another, and she cried out, pulling Chad down to her, crushing her breasts beneath the heavy mass of his chest, grateful for the solid anchor of his body to cling to. As Tucker called out from the dark waters that engulfed her, Chad let the final edge of his control slip, and she saw release flood his face as they plunged together down into the deep oblivion of satisfaction.

When Tucker opened her eyes, Chad shifted to his side and drew her close to him, and they lay quietly for a long time, still joined together, their bodies damp with the shared sweat of their efforts. Their breathing slowed down to a relaxed pace. The silence between them was comfortable, filled with intimacy and trust. Tucker nuzzled into the hollow of Chad's shoulder, and he stroked her hair tenderly.

Her mind was a peaceful haze of sensation: the feel of Chad's solid body against hers, the new earthy fragrance of their individual scents blended into one, the far-away roar of the sea.

Chad reached up and clicked off the lamp beside the bed. Moonlight pooled on the shiny wood floor, filling the room with the palest hint of blue light. Tucker heard Chad's breathing become deep and even, and as she counted his breaths, wondering if he were asleep, she slipped off into her own peaceful slumber.

_____ ELEVEN _____

The first thing Tucker became aware of was the smell of fresh coffee. Her eyes were still closed when the distinctive aroma slid into her dreamy consciousness and slowly eased her into wakefulness. She stretched, and her body ached with a pleasant awareness of itself, a tangible reminder of the night before. Still only half awake, her legs reached across the bed, instinctively searching for Chad, but found only cold sheets. She opened her eyes.

Sunlight trickled into her bedroom, bathing the familiar room in the pale glow of very early morning. Fully awake now, she sat up straight. The door to the bathroom was ajar and the light off. Chad was nowhere in sight. A disturbing thought cut through her. Had he left her alone without even saying goodbye? Had last night meant so little to him?

She was naked, and feeling suddenly vulnerable, she gathered the sheets about her protectively as she looked around the room. She saw her clothes, still pooled on the shiny floor where she had dropped them. It seemed a thousand years ago she had taken them off.

"Good morning."

Chad stood in the doorway, two steaming coffee mugs in hand. He had pulled on his jeans, which rode low on his hips, but nothing else. An overnight growth of beard darkened his strong jawline.

"Good morning." That was all she was able to say. He was as magnificent as she remembered. Tucker's mind was flooded with vivid images of the night before, and she felt a warm flush color her cheeks.

"I made coffee. You're out of milk, and I couldn't find the sugar. Is black okay?" He stayed in the doorway, as if waiting for some sign from her, some indication that it was okay for him to enter the room.

"Black's great." It seemed quite peculiar to be talking about something as ordinary as coffee with Chad after what had happened between them last night, but she didn't know what else to say.

Chad put both mugs down on the bedside table, then he leaned over and kissed her, slowly and thoroughly, and the spicy warmth of his mouth sent the echo of remembered sensations all through her body. Unrestrained by conscious thought, her body responded to him and Tucker returned the kiss with a sudden burst of passion.

Chad's brows shot up in pleased surprise. "Good morning, again." He gathered the pillows together and plumped them behind her so she could lean back against them. He sat on the side of the bed, looking at her, a gentle, enigmatic smile on his face. She waited a full minute for him to speak. When he didn't, she did.

"Chad."

"Yes?" He continued to look at her, seriously now, as if patiently studying her features for a portrait.

"I could really use that coffee."

"Oh, yeah, right." He handed her one mug and he took the other. For a long moment, they each sipped in silence. Tucker studied Chad surreptitiously over the rim of her mug. He seemed preoccupied. Of course, she probably did, too. Was it just the normal jitters for two lovers on their first morning after? Not that she would know. She had never been in this kind of a situation before.

Then she remembered. Chad had other things on his mind besides what had happened between them last night. Jamie was coming today.

"I don't have too much time. The plane gets in at eight," he said, as if he had read her mind.

Chad took her hand and held it silently for a moment, big fingers gently massaging her palm. "But I don't want to leave you."

"You don't have to." She squeezed his hand, returning the pleasant pressure.

"What do you mean?"

"If it's all right with you, I would really like to go with you to meet Jamie."

The gratitude she read on his face told her more clearly than any words how much he wanted her there with him, and for some reason, that touched her deeply. He smiled and kissed her quickly, once, and then again.

"I would like that very much," was all he said. He took her empty mug from her hand. "I'll take care of these and give you some privacy."

He stopped in the door and looked back. "I haven't said it yet. Thank you for last night. I mean for what you said to me." He hesitated, and for a moment Tucker saw the boy in a man's body. "I guess I mean everything, really." He ran a hand through his sleep-ruffled hair. "You're a remarkable woman." He smiled and closed the bedroom door behind him.

Tucker leaned back against the pillows and smiled to herself. Chad didn't realize what a milestone last night had been for her. She hadn't been with a man since Peter, and she had never wanted to. But Chad was different. Something had happened to her last night, some final stage of healing that she had been waiting for. It was as if she had passed through a door and shut it behind her, never to return. For that, she would always be grateful to Chad.

The thought she couldn't face was that this was all temporary. She went into the bathroom and turned on the shower. After Jamie was sent back to the mainland, Joshua's estate settled and the shop sold, he would be gone, and Chad Carver would be a closed chapter of her life. She shook her head to try to clear the thought away, and stepped into the shower.

Tucker's tiny red pickup wound its way over the ten miles of road to the Airport-in-the-Sky. Chad was at the wheel, and Tucker beside him on the bench seat. He skillfully maneuvered the truck over the narrow, twisting road bordered by tall eucalyptus trees that brought them deeper into Catalina's interior. With each switchback, they climbed higher and higher to the two hills near the island's center. When they reached the airport nearly forty-five minutes later, they parked the truck and got out.

The morning was clear and bright, and the view over the rolling hills to the blue Pacific was spectacular. A few private planes were tied down on the asphalt, and a regular commuter charter was preparing for take-off, but otherwise the airport was quiet.

At the edge of the asphalt field, Chad turned around slowly, surveying the horizon for 360 degrees. The skies were empty. He checked his watch.

"Jamie's not due for another fifteen minutes or so. Do you want to get another cup of coffee?" Chad took her hand as they approached the terminal building with an easy familiarity that she liked.

"Okay. The Runway Cafe is open." Tucker spotted a table in the sun on the red-tiled patio. They took seats and ordered. After the waitress had left, Tucker asked "Does it seem strange to you, talking about him?"

Chad looked thoughtful. "You mean Jamie?"

"Yes. We keep saying things like, 'Jamie will be here this morning' and 'I hope Jamie's plane isn't late,' like he's just a regular part of your life. I mean, not only have you never met him, up until a few days ago, you didn't even know he existed."

"You're right, it is strange." Chad traced an invisible pattern on the well-worn tabletop. "It's very, very strange. I don't really know how to explain it. But ever since I found out, I feel like there's this other piece of me out there that I don't know anything about."

The waitress brought their coffee. Chad stared into his steaming mug for a moment. "Tucker, my mother's dead. My father's dead. I thought I was totally alone. And now, out of nowhere there's this other person. He's my brother, and I want to know him.''

A small commuter plane appeared on the horizon. They finished their coffee in silence as they watched the plane make its approach. Tucker noticed that Chad followed the plane's progress very closely, never taking his gaze from it. She couldn't read the emotion that she saw glowing in his eyes.

The plane touched down on the short runway, and turned to taxi to its unloading position. Chad dropped some money on the table and stood up.

"I guess this is it." He kissed Tucker quickly on the cheek. "Thank you for being here with me." She squeezed his hand firmly in response. She could feel the tension in his fingers.

The ground crew rolled the portable steps up to the door of the plane. Two couples were first off, followed by two men with large packages. Chad and Tucker approached the plane, pausing about ten yards away, waiting. No other passengers appeared for what seemed like minutes, and Tucker wondered if maybe they had the wrong time.

She was about to say something to Chad when a small boy appeared from the hatch at the top of the stairs. He was wearing a dark blue backpack and carrying a cheap-looking suitcase. He paused at the top of the stairs and looked out over the few people waiting on the asphalt below. He shielded his eyes against the morning sun, as if to see better. Tucker's heart twisted within her, knowing that he would never see the man he was looking for.

The little boy started down the steps. He was blond, and looked very much like his pictures, but smaller and slighter than Tucker had imagined him. He wore a red T-shirt and jeans that were too short for him.

Chad started walking toward the plane to meet him at the bottom of the steps. Tucker hung back a little, not wanting to intrude in a private moment, and also unsure how Chad would handle the situation.

Chad walked slowly. He needed every second to choose his words. Even though he had been over the situation in his mind a dozen times, now he felt no closer to knowing what to say. The funny thing was, he was not a man who was used to being uncertain about what to do or say. Today he felt as skittish and confused as he could ever remember.

Jamie paused halfway down the steps, looking again for Joshua. His face was detached, distant, almost stoic. Most people would think it was an odd expression for a little boy, but not Chad. He recognized the expression on the boy's face immediately, and the recognition wrenched his guts.

This was the face of false bravery, the face of

a child who has seen through the lies of the adult world, and who now dares the world to try to lie to him again. This was the face that covered fear, and anger, and despair. He knew the face. This was the face that stared back defiantly from dozens of pictures of his own childhood.

The boy, obviously not recognizing anyone, descended the rest of the steps. He reached the asphalt and paused, apparently uncertain where to go.

"Jamie?" Chad stopped and waited. *Don't scare him off. Let him decide when he's ready to answer.* He was willing to wait.

Jamie turned toward him slowly, his mask of uninterest firmly in place. "Yeah?"

"I'm Chad." He gestured Tucker to his side. She stepped in closer. "This is Tucker. We're friends of your—" He paused. Suddenly referring to Joshua as someone else's father seemed very strange. He started again. "We're friends of Joshua's."

Jamie looked suspicious. "So where is he? He's supposed to meet me here." He looked behind them, toward the terminal. "Is he inside?"

"Jamie." Chad knelt down on one knee, bringing him to the boy's height. "There's no point in dragging this out. I've got to tell you some bad news." Chad put a hand on the boy's shoulder.

Chad saw Jamie's indifference slip slightly. "What? What happened? Did he decide he didn't

want me?" He shrugged Chad's hand off his
shoulder. "No problem. I can go back. This
wasn't my idea, you know." He gripped the handle of his suitcase more tightly, and his knuckles
whitened. "If he doesn't want me to live here,
that's fine with me."

Chad felt his gut tighten with anguish for the
boy. He took a deep breath, unsure how to proceed. He looked to Tucker for a brief moment.
He was grateful for her presence here with him;
he kept his eyes locked onto hers until he felt
them pass some of their calm to him. He took
another deep breath, and went on. "Jamie, that's
not what's happened." Chad cleared his throat,
trying to get rid of the thickness growing in his
voice.

"Joshua wanted you here. He wanted that very,
very much. But he's not here with us today.
Jamie, he had a heart attack. He's dead."

For a few brief seconds, Chad saw shock, followed by total despair, flash across the boy's face.
For those few seconds, he looked like a very
frightened little boy, all alone in the world. But
then just as quickly as it came, the moment of
raw emotion passed from his eyes, and the cool
detachment returned.

"Oh." He scuffed the toe of his sneaker against
the asphalt. "When?"

"Two months ago. It happened very suddenly.
I'm sorry to have to tell you this. You should have

been told earlier. It must be hard for you to hear it this way." Chad didn't try to put his hand back on Jamie's shoulder. He guessed that underneath the boy's cool attitude, an emotional storm was raging.

"I only met him twice. It's not like he was— it's not like he was really like my father or anything. I didn't want to move to this stupid island anyway. I've got friends. I've got things to do." He checked the straps of his backpack, as if he were afraid he'd lost something. "I can go back to my foster parents, you know."

"I'm sure you can."

"They'll be glad. They didn't want me to leave. They're really cool. They'll be really glad to have me back."

Jamie's enthusiasm for his foster family rung slightly false, but Chad decided to let that subject drop. "Anyway, I'm sorry about what's happened. I'd like to help you if I could, maybe—"

Jamie cut him off. "It's no big deal. I'm okay." He stared belligerently at Chad as if daring him to continue trying to talk to him.

Chad stood in silence, feeling helpless in the face of the boy's denial of his feelings. He looked at Tucker briefly, then switched tactics.

"You've never been to Catalina before, right?"

Jamie sullenly shook his head.

"Well, since you're already here, maybe you

would like to see the island." *Come on, kid. At least give me a chance.*

"No, I don't think so." He tugged at the straps of his backpack again. "I should probably just go back right now. I've got things to do."

"Tucker and I know some pretty cool places. Why don't you stay overnight with us? You can go back tomorrow."

"No, I'm gonna go back right now." Jamie slowly surveyed the dusty brown hills encircling the tiny airport. "This place stinks."

Tucker looked to Chad for his response, but he was silent. She read the frustration in his eyes. Should she say something to Jamie?

She knelt down beside him. "Jamie, please stay with us for the day. We can—"

He turned icy blue eyes on her. "Forget it. You're not my mom. You can't make me stay here."

Jamie picked up his suitcase, turned, and started walking quickly back toward the asphalt field. He stopped suddenly. The plane he had arrived on was taxiing to the opposite end of the runway. Jamie yelled and waved, "Hey! Wait up!"

The plane turned slowly around to begin its takeoff. The twin engines roared, and the plane began to move down the runway, rapidly accelerating. Jamie started running toward the plane, frantically waving his free arm. "Wait for me!" Now he was a few steps from the plane's path.

He dropped his suitcase and stepped out on the runway, waving both his arms.

Tucker's heart was pounding with sudden fear. "Jamie, no! Get back!" She ordered her legs to move, but she felt glued to the dirt.

Chad sprinted by her shoulder, nearly knocking her to the ground. In a few long strides he was beside Jamie on the runway. The pilot, shocked by the sudden appearance of the boy in his path, cut his engines, but the forward momentum of the plane continued to carry him down the runway toward the two people in his way.

"Oh my God, Chad!" Tucker's scream melded with the high-pitched squeal of brakes that split the air as the pilot tried to stop the plane.

Chad tackled Jamie and rolled them both out of the path of the plane's landing gear, which came within a few feet of rolling over both of them. The plane finally came to a stop thirty feet further down the blacktop. Tucker breathed a silent prayer of thanks and ran to meet them.

Chad carried Jamie back to the edge of the blacktop and put him down. "That was an incredibly stupid thing to do, kid." He rubbed his elbow, scraped raw from the asphalt. "You nearly got us both killed."

Jamie sat down on his suitcase, shaking. His jeans were torn at the knee. "I'm sorry. I'm really sorry. I-I thought he could stop." He put his face in his hands, and Tucker and Chad exchanged looks. *This boy is so upset he can't think straight,* she thought to herself. *I don't think Chad knows what he's getting into.*

"If you're so anxious to get back, maybe what I ought to do is put you on another plane right now." Chad's voice was rough, but Tucker felt his concern beneath the anger.

Jamie looked up, waiting. He wiped his nose with the back of his hand.

"But since you're still here, my offer stands."

Jamie seemed to have regained a bit of his cool attitude. He stood up and shrugged. "If you still want to. Doesn't make any difference to me."

Tucker waited for Chad's temper to flare, but instead he just reached for Jamie's suitcase. "Come on," he said, arching an eyebrow pointedly at Tucker. "It'll be fun."

"Yeah, sure, whatever you say," said Jamie. He looked doubtful, but let Chad take the suitcase. The three walked back to the truck in silence.

Tucker wondered what Chad had in mind. Chad put Jamie's meager belongings in the bed of the truck. He motioned Tucker in first. "Let Jamie take the window." She slid in next to Chad. The solid warmth of his denim-clad thigh felt good pressed against hers. He put his hand on her leg in a gesture both possessive and reassuring. Without thinking, her hand captured his and kept it there.

Jamie took the window, next to Tucker. He sat

as far away as possible, pressed up against the door with his arm out the open window. His expression was somewhere between boredom and disgust. *I hope you've got something good up your sleeve, Chad. This is one tough little customer here.* She didn't have to wait long.

They pulled out of the airport. When they reached the fork in the road that was the turnoff from the main road to the airport, Chad did not take the left turn toward Avalon as Tucker had expected. Instead, he went the other direction, taking the dirt road that wound deeper into the island's interior.

Tucker looked at Chad and arched her eyebrows in a silent question. He smiled mysteriously and said, "I thought you and Jamie might like to see something you'll never see on the mainland."

Jamie said nothing. He just stared out the window, looking bored. Tucker wondered what was going through the little boy's mind; his eyes seemed so much older than the rest of his features. She wondered what those eyes had seen that made them that way.

The little truck climbed up and down a series of hills, each a little higher than the last. Catalina's interior was a rugged, dry landscape of mountains and valleys, crisscrossed only by a few dirt roads and trails. Each time they reached a peak, spectacular vistas of the Pacific came into view.

"What do you think of the island so far, Jamie?" Tucker tried to break the awkward silence.

Jamie shrugged. "Looks like a lot of nothing to me. Where are the people? Where's the city?"

"Most of them live in Avalon, which is more of a town than a city, and a few more families live down in Two Harbors." Chad gestured toward the Pacific side of the island. "But nobody lives here in the interior. Just the animals."

Tucker noticed that Jamie was now watching with guarded interest. "What kind of animals?" The little boy kept his voice cool and uninterested.

"You'll see."

Suddenly, as they were nearly to the top of the highest hill they had yet reached, Chad pulled the truck off the narrow road. He shut off the engine and hopped out.

"Why are we stopping?" asked Tucker.

Chad stuck his head through the open window and smiled. "Wait and see."

Jamie, visibly intrigued, opened his door and scrambled out, leaving the door wide open behind. Tucker quickly followed him.

Chad had struck out ahead on a narrow trail that cut through the wild sage and scrub oak. She and Jamie nearly had to run to catch up to him. The trail was so narrow that they had to walk single file. What was Chad being so mysterious about?

The grade became steeper, and Tucker's sneakers slipped a bit in the loose dirt. She stopped to get her balance back. Chad and Jamie kept going, moving quickly up the steep path.

Up ahead, the trail flattened out at the crest of the hill. Chad reached the top first, with Jamie close behind him. They stopped abruptly, looking over at something on the other side of the ridge.

"Wow!" Jamie spoke quietly, his voice filled with something approaching reverence. Chad stood in silence, staring down. Tucker scrambled up the final few feet to see what they were looking at.

The other side of the hill fell away sharply in a sheer vertical drop of nearly seventy-five feet. At the base of the cliff was a meadow, with a small watering hole that was bordered by a grove of cottonwoods. Gathered around the watering hole was a herd of buffalo.

Tucker held her breath. They were magnificent animals, with huge heads and massive shaggy bodies. Tucker knew that despite their size, each one more than 2,000 pounds, the animals could outrun a racehorse—not to mention a person. Their sharp horns looked dangerous, but the beasts' big eyes were surprisingly gentle. She had seen Catalina's buffalo before, but never as many as this, and never at such close range. She estimated the herd at between fifty and sixty.

"How did they get out here?" Jamie was visibly thrilled by the enormous animals. All signs of the boy's cool demeanor had evaporated at the sight of the herd.

"They were brought here on a boat, or their ancestors were anyway, back in the late twenties for a movie." Chad spoke in hushed tones, as if the animals might overhear them.

"A movie? What do you mean?" Jamie answered in the same heavy whisper that Chad used.

"They filmed it here on the island. It was a western called *The Vanishing American*. The movie people brought over fourteen buffalo. After the filming was done, it was too hard to round them up again, so they just left them to run free. Now there are about five hundred of them here in the interior of the island."

"Wow! Just like cowboys and Indians." Jamie's eyes were shining with exciting ideas. "They're huge. Do they ever stampede?"

"No, I don't think so. But every couple of years, a bull gets separated from his herd and finds his way into town. It's not easy to round up one of these big guys and get him back into the interior where he belongs."

"Have you ever done that?" Jamie asked.

Chad smiled, a wave of memory passing over his features. "Once, yes, I helped get this one old bull back through the gate. It was really something. I was only a couple years older than you are now."

"What happened?" Jamie was listening, but he kept his eyes on the buffalo below.

"He must have wandered into town very early in the morning, before it was light. This old lady on Whitley Avenue looked out her window, and saw this big old bull in her front yard. She called the police, but by the time they got there he had trotted down to Crescent—that's the street that runs right by the town beach. The police chased him through town with the siren going, and he got really spooked. He ended up on the golf course by the elementary school. A bunch of us kids chased him up and down the length of the golf course about five times until he finally went through the gate. I think he was pretty glad to get away from all that noise."

"Cool." Jamie looked at Chad with new interest. Tucker smiled at the image that formed in her mind: Chad as a boy, whooping and yelling, waving his arms wildly as he chased a nervous buffalo back to safety.

The three of them stood in silence for a few minutes, taking in the primitive beauty of the scene before them. Tucker felt once again the wildness of the island that had drawn her here, the feeling of separation from the rest of the civilized world that had given her solace. This untamed sense of nature was the essence of Catalina, not the restaurants and bars and T-shirt shops of Avalon. This was the feeling she had sought and found here. She gratefully drank it in again.

Jamie broke the silence. He was bouncing a little with the excitement. "What else lives back in here?"

"Well, there're goats, foxes, wild boars, and some deer."

"Wow! I don't ever see any animals at home, except one time, when I went to the zoo."

Tucker and Chad exchanged looks over Jamie's head. Tucker wondered where Jamie now considered home. His latest foster parents' house? The family before them? The one-bedroom apartment in Long Beach where he and Darlene had been living at the time of her death?

The three stood without speaking for a few minutes, watching the enormous animals graze. Finally Chad broke the silence. "Okay, the tour bus is leaving." Chad offered his hand to Tucker as they descended the steep trail back down to the car. Jamie lingered behind a moment, watching the herd.

"Chad," Tucker kept her voice low, "is that really true? Did you really chase a buffalo?"

Chad smiled. "Of course I did. Did you think it was just a lot of bull?"

Tucker groaned in response. "Oh, Chad. Really." She grabbed him and kissed him suddenly. He seized the opportunity to pull her close to him for a moment, and she relished the feeling of his hard body against her own. They kissed one more time, and Tucker felt desire start to swell within her.

"Whoa, we'd better be respectable with the kid along," said Chad, but the gleam in his eye told her that he felt the same surge of longing that she did.

Jamie caught up with them at the truck. "So where are we going next?" His voice was cool, but Tucker could hear an undercurrent of enthusiasm that hadn't been there earlier. Whether he liked it or not, Jamie was responding to Catalina, and to Chad.

Chad opened the passenger door to the truck to let Tucker slide in. "How do you feel about pirates?"

"Pirates? You're putting me on." Jamie looked at Chad with skepticism. Tucker's face mirrored Jamie's expression.

"If you're not interested in buried treasure, we don't have to go." Chad walked around to the driver's side with exaggerated nonchalance.

"Where? Go where? I'm ready." Jamie scrambled in next to Tucker and slammed the door. "Come on, let's go. I want to see everything."

The rest of the day passed in a blur of activities. Tucker was amazed at the range of Chad's knowledge of the island, and his pleasure at sharing it with her and Jamie was obvious.

At Two Harbors, they all went swimming in the clear water of the bay. After drying off, they had an impromptu lunch on the beach. Chad regaled them with stories of pirates, and buried treasure, and the men who had given twenty years or more of their lives to an unsuccessful search for the legendary wealth that was hidden on the island.

Back in Avalon, Chad took them on a walking tour of the town. Some of the homes they stopped to look at were more than one hundred years old, and Chad seemed to know a story for each one of them. Some of the stories were funny and some were sad, but Chad told them all with an infectious enthusiasm that swept them into the time he spoke about. Tucker was thrilled to learn so much about places she had walked by nearly every day for the last six years.

After a stop at the grocery store, their walk finally brought them to Joshua's house as the late afternoon began turning into dusk.

Dinner was a joint effort. Tucker took charge of the spaghetti sauce, leaving the salad and garlic bread for Chad and Jamie. Tucker watched from her station at the stove as Chad showed Jamie how to wash and tear the lettuce, and peel the garlic with a small knife.

Chad was very different with Jamie than she had expected. All day long she had been surprised by his relaxed manner and his patience. Even during Jamie's more obstinate moments earlier in the day, he had remained calm. His delight in sharing the island had been contagious, and Tucker had learned quite a few things she didn't know.

"What was it like here when you were my age?" Jamie mopped up the last of the spaghetti sauce with some bread. He had eaten an enormous amount of food. Tucker marveled that one little boy could hold so much.

Chad sat back in his chair. His eyes searched the ceiling, picking out memories. "It was a lot like it is now, but a lot quieter. Not as many people visited, and not as many people lived on the island." He took a sip of wine, lost for the moment in a private thought.

Tucker quietly cleared away the plates. She knew that many of Chad's memories were too tarnished with pain to repeat. Yet today, none of that had been evident. He had only conveyed to Jamie a sense of wonder and joy about the island.

"You know, Jamie, if I remember right, Joshua had some great old pictures of the island. Some of the really old ones he got from his father." Chad wandered over to the deep bookshelves that flanked the fireplace. "They used to be somewhere around here."

Everything had been virtually the same as he had remembered it from growing up. The occasional feeling of déjà vu had been overwhelming. He ran his hand over the dusty spines. Sure enough, here were the three big leather albums that he remembered. He pulled them out and stacked them on the coffee table.

Jamie joined him on the couch while Tucker started coffee. He opened the first one. "Here we go. This is the Casino while it was under construction. That was in 1929."

"Are there slot machines there?"

Chad and Tucker exchanged amused glances. "No, but a lot of people ask about that. There's never been any gambling on the island, even though we call this building the Casino. Casino just means 'a gathering place' in Italian. There's a movie theater downstairs, and a ballroom for dancing upstairs, but it's nothing like Las Vegas."

Jamie eagerly flipped through the rest of the album's pages, asking questions. Chad started looking at the next book, looking for particular photos he remembered.

"Why are these people going swimming wearing their clothes?" asked Jamie, wrinkling his nose quizzically.

Tucker came in to join them. "What?" She sat down on the couch on the other side of Jamie. "Who's swimming in their clothes?"

"Look." Jamie pointed to the picture of the crowd of tourists in their old-fashioned bathing costumes. "They look really silly."

Chad laughed. "That's what people wore to the beach back then." He smiled at Tucker over

Jamie's head. "Think your friend would sell many of these in her bikini shop?"

"Not likely."

Jamie reached the end of the first book. "What's this?" He held up two bundles of envelopes. "They were stuck in the back."

Chad took the bundles from Jamie's hand, and examined the thicker bunch. Fastened together with a rubber band were letters addressed to Joshua in a strong hand, twenty or more. The writing on the envelopes was very familiar. Chad recognized it as his own.

He slowly flipped through the stack, looking at the postmarks, a parade of half-remembered names—all the places he had been for the last ten years. He always wrote, only once, just to let his father know he was still alive. He'd never expected a reply, and he'd never received one. His stomach felt like a deep pit of despair.

"Chad, what is it?" Tucker's eyes carried a concern her voice did not reveal. She glanced cautiously toward Jamie, but he had lost interest in the letters and was buried in the next album.

"These are my letters to Joshua." Chad cleared his throat. "Looks like every letter I ever wrote to him. He must have saved them all." He didn't remember writing this many letters. He looked through the second stack.

The second set was not the same. There were only six in this stack, and these envelopes were blank. Curious, Chad opened the first one. Inside was a letter written in his father's handwriting.

Dear Chad,
   This is the hardest letter I have ever had to write. I hope you will read it, even though I would understand if you threw it away without reading another word, when you saw it was from me. Believe me, I know you have good reason to hate me.

Chad stopped in shock. He had never received this letter. Looking further, he saw the letter stopped halfway down the page, obviously unfinished. He opened the next envelope.

Dear Chad,
   How are you son? I pray to God every day that you are okay and happy where you are. Please try and read this letter and see if you can find it in your heart to forgive your father for the mistakes he has made in his life. I can only pray—

This one ended abruptly as well. Chad stood up, keeping both sets of envelopes with him. "I think I better get some air." Jamie looked at him curiously, but went back to the photo albums.
   Tucker stood up. "Chad, is everything okay? Are you feeling all right?" She touched him

lightly on the arm. The feeling of her hand steadied his nerves.

"I'm fine. I'm going out to the porch. I just need to be alone for a few minutes." Chad glanced significantly at Jamie, then back to Tucker. She nodded, receiving his meaning.

"Okay. I'll just finish up in the kitchen. Do you want me to bring your coffee out there?"

"Yes, that would be good."

Jamie was still engrossed in the thick albums. Chad moved slowly to the front porch, his mind a jumble of memories and conjectures. The night was cool, much cooler than it had been since he had arrived back on Catalina. He stood silently, looking up at the moon for a moment, then turned his attention back to the letters. Most were false starts, like the first two, but he finally came to one that was nearly complete.

Dear Chad,

This is the hardest letter I have ever had to write, but I must do it. My sponsor says that the Ninth Step was hell for him, too, but that's not making it any easier. You are the only one left that I haven't made amends to, and God knows you are the most important.

Chad, I am an alcoholic. I have not had a drink for more than a year and a half now, but I am still an alcoholic, and will be for the rest of my life. I thank God every day for my sobriety, and for the program of Alcoholics Anonymous that helps me keep it. I only wish that I could have found it years ago; maybe things between us would be different now.

I was a terrible father to you, Chad. No one else knows that as well as I do now. I hurt you. I abused you. I depended on you to take care of me, more than you probably even realize. I took advantage of you, and I was never there for you. I know that now. Now that the booze is out of my system, I see a lot of things more clearly.

I loved you, Chad, I really did, but after your mother died, I couldn't find a way to tell you. Sometimes it seemed as if my love for you had all dried up inside me. Sometimes it hurt me just to see you. You were so much like her, I couldn't let myself love you the way you deserved. It was easier to ignore you. I drank to take away the pain of losing Irene, but it always came back. I ate and drank self-pity every single day. Those were dark days.

Darlene was the first bright spot in my life since Irene died. Does that surprise you? I had been so lonely. I loved her, Chad. I really loved her. You probably didn't realize it, but she was very good-hearted.

After you left the island, we found out that

Darlene was pregnant. I asked her to marry me. She refused. She told me that she believed I was an alcoholic, and unless I quit drinking, she would never marry me. She had a drinking problem, too, although she didn't think so at the time.

Of course, she was right, but I wouldn't admit it. I told her she could go to hell, I didn't need her and her temperance lectures. If she really loved me, she wouldn't care if I had a little too much sometimes. She left me and went back to the mainland. I felt bad as hell for a long time, but we still kept in touch with each other. I sent her money for the baby every month, and I kept hoping that someday she would come back to me, and bring the little boy, too, and we could be together again. Unfortunately, that hope wasn't enough to get me sober.

Well, a year and a half ago, Darlene was killed in a car accident, and that damn near killed me, too. I'd lost the only two women I had ever loved, and my son was gone for good as well. I coped with the pain the same way I always had, and I tied one on. I was drunk for weeks. One night during that time I went out to the boat for some fool reason I can't remember, and I fell getting back into the dinghy and hit my head on the side of the boat. Lucky for me the harbor patrol saw me fall, and fished me out before I went under for good. The fellow who saved me came by the house to check on me the next day. Turns out he was in the Program, and that night he took me to my first meeting. And that was how I got my second chance.

After I'd been sober a couple of months, I got the idea that I should try and get custody of Jamie; that is Darlene's little boy. I've been working on it for more than a year now, but it hasn't come through yet. There's a lot of red tape to something like this. I'm not giving up, though. I don't want to lose Jamie the same way I lost you, Chad. I don't know if we can ever get over this terrible hurt between us, but Jamie's still a little boy. Maybe there's still time for him and me to have some time together.

Anyway, Chad, this is all probably a lot to swallow at one time. I've been trying to get this all down on paper for quite a while now, but every time I try I end up giving up. It just seems too hard. Maybe I can make it work this time. If I could only talk to you, see you face to face just once, maybe we could talk things through. God knows I want to.

A few more lines followed, scratched out to be illegible, then the letter ended. There was no signature. Chad leaned against the porch rail for support and took several deep breaths. The past and the present were all jumbled up in his mind, a surrealistic blend of memories. He jumped like a skittish cat when the screen door banged shut.

Tucker put the steaming coffee mugs down on the wide porch railing before she spoke. "Jamie's already asleep on the couch. He must have drifted off while I was in the kitchen. I just threw a blanket over him. He's pretty beat. He's had quite a few things to deal with today." She slipped her arm around Chad's waist.

Chad smiled ruefully. "Yeah, I know how he feels." Silently he handed Tucker the letter he had just read. She read it slowly, twice, before she said anything. She felt Joshua's suffering behind every word, felt how dearly each line must have cost him. Yet he had never been able to send it, never quite been able to get the words on paper to fully convey what was in his heart.

"Chad, I never realized how bad Joshua's problem was." She looked back down at the page. "He went through a lot of pain in his life." Tucker waited, wondering what Chad's reaction to the letter would be. He seemed strangely calm; she wondered what it was about him that seemed different.

"Yes, he did." Chad leaned forward with a loud exhalation of breath, his forearms resting on the rough wooden railing. He stared out into the night, silent for a long time. Tucker listened to his breathing, waiting for him to continue.

"You know, I never really thought much about what it must have been like for him when my mother died. I know how it was for me. Somehow, I guess I never thought it could possibly have been as rough for anyone other than me." Chad's eyes were distant. "He must have been so lonely. We never once talked about it. All I ever thought about was me."

"Chad, you were a child then. It was normal for you to be focused on yourself. You had to be to survive. Don't chastise yourself for that. You did the best you could."

"I guess I believe that. But these letters make me wish my dad and I could have talked about this; maybe it would have been easier for both of us."

"Maybe so." Tucker rubbed his back in a gentle rhythm of comfort. "But we can't change the past, no matter how much we might like to."

"Yeah. That's sure as hell true." They were both silent for a while, lost in thought. Chad's eyes narrowed slightly, as if he were closing in on an elusive idea. "But Joshua changed himself, didn't he?"

"You mean he quit drinking."

"That's right. I never thought he would be able to do it, but he did. I've got to give him that. And he did his best to take care of Jamie, too."

"Chad, Joshua made a lot of mistakes, that's for sure, but I think you still have a couple of good reasons to be proud of your father."

Chad looked at her for a long moment, working some unknown thought out. "You're right. I never in my life thought I would say it, but I am proud of him. It's a good feeling." He kissed her softly, a comforting touch of one soul seeking and finding another. "Let's go inside."

TWELVE

"Damn it, all I'm asking is for you to let us have him for a couple of days. He just got here yesterday."

Tucker could hear Chad's patience growing thin. He had decided last night to ask the child welfare authorities for permission to keep Jamie with them for a few days when he called to explain about Joshua's death.

Now it was nearly 8:30, and he had been on the phone in the kitchen for nearly half an hour. At first, he'd been passed from department to department, trying to locate the social worker who was handling Jamie's case. Finally, it seemed as though he was talking to the right person; but so far, from what she could hear, his request for

Jamie to stay on Catalina for even one more day
had been flatly denied.

Tucker was slumped in an overstuffed chair in
the living room, looking out the window, watching
for Jamie. Before Chad placed the call, she had
sent the boy off to the boardwalk with some raw
hamburger and a few crackers to feed the crabs.
She didn't want him to walk in while Chad was
still on the phone. He had already been through
enough upheaval in the last twenty-four hours.

"—I told you already, I'm his brother, for
God's sake. I know I'm not in your file, but I
don't see why you can't let him have a few days
here." Chad was silent, apparently listening to
whoever was on the other end of the phone.
"Well, is there someone else I can talk to about
this? What about his foster parents? Jamie seems
to get along with them pretty well."

Tucker came back into the kitchen. Chad was
standing defiantly, legs spread wide, feet planted
firmly. "That's the stupidest thing I've ever—"
He ran a hand through his hair in a gesture of
frustration. "I see. No, I understand what you're
saying, I just don't see—"

He listened for a long time without speaking.
Then the air suddenly seemed to go out of him,
and he sagged into one of the chairs around the
ancient dining room table. His voice became flat
and expressionless. "I understand. I'll get him
there by noon." He hung up the phone, and

rubbed the heel of his hand against his forehead, as if fighting a headache.

"They wouldn't budge?" She hated seeing him look so defeated.

"Not an inch. When his case worker found out about Joshua, she nearly flipped. First she tried to tell me that it couldn't have happened, that all placements were re-verified by phone before the child was released; that is standard procedure." Chad smiled grimly. "I explained to her that Jamie was here on the island, and Joshua Carver was dead regardless of whether it followed their procedures or not."

"Chad, what's going to happen to him?" She sat down at the table next to him.

"I'm supposed to put him on the next plane back to Long Beach. I guess I could refuse, but as his case worker pointed out a number of times, I don't even have the legal right to have him here with me right now. She didn't exactly threaten me, but by the end of the conversation she made it pretty clear that the authorities would consider my keeping Jamie here on Catalina tantamount to abduction."

"What? That's absolutely ridiculous!" Tucker couldn't believe what she was hearing. "It's not like you kidnapped him!"

"I know, but they're the ones who screwed up by sending him here, and I think she's probably just trying to cover her own tail. She told me to get him on the next plane, and she would have someone meet his flight on the mainland and take him to Lemonwood."

"Lemonwood? What's that?" Although she couldn't place it, the name struck her with cold familiarity, as if it were a place she had known in another part of her life, long ago.

"It's a temporary facility for children who are wards of the state. He'll be there until they can place him somewhere else long term."

"I don't understand. I thought his foster parents would be taking him back to live with them. That's what Jamie's planning on."

"Unfortunately, it doesn't work that way. He lost his spot with his foster family when he received his permanent placement with Joshua. His space there has already been filled with another child. He has to wait until another spot becomes available."

"Chad." Tucker felt tears forming in her eyes. She gestured silently toward the back door. His gaze followed hers. There by the door were Jamie's few possessions: a sad-looking suitcase and a stained backpack, packed and waiting to move on. "I feel so awful about this."

"So do I, Tucker. So do I."

Chad stood, and she was in his arms. His strong arms wrapped her in a reassuring cocoon of warmth, holding her close to his chest. She wished she could stay burrowed inside there forever. They stood together, comforting each other for several minutes.

Tucker felt wetness on her face, and in that moment she realized she wasn't just crying for Jamie, she was crying for herself, too; not for the loss of the past, but for the loss that was yet to come.

She loved Chad Carver. That realization was sudden and sharp and painful. After she had lost Peter, she had thought the part of her that could love a man and give herself completely to him had died with her husband. She had been grateful to have truly loved one man in her life, and she was certain there would never be another one.

But she had been wrong. She had been caught unaware. Chad had dared her to care again, challenged her to try again. Something in Chad had spoken to her pain and loss, and moved her beyond them to a new level of forgiveness and healing. She had fallen in love with Chad, and soon she would be losing him forever.

They found Jamie past the Tuna Club, on the rocks below the boardwalk leading to the Casino. They stood together, watching him for a while before he saw them. Jamie scrambled over the rocks with the assurance of a boy who had spent his whole life on these beaches. Tucker smiled as she watched him carefully place a tiny morsel of the hamburger in a crevice of the rock, and back up slightly to wait for the crabs to attack. He laughed with delight when two of the tiny creatures decided to do battle over the bit of food.

"He doesn't look like a city boy at all, does he?" Chad spoke softly, as if thinking out loud, but keeping his eyes on Jamie.

"No, he doesn't." Tucker slipped her hand into Chad's. "Of course, neither does his brother." She squeezed his hand tightly, and he returned the pressure. "Chad, I know it's none of my business, but . . ."

"What?"

"Don't you think you should tell Jamie who you really are?"

Chad put his foot up on the short wall that edged the boardwalk, watching Jamie "I don't know. How do you think he would feel about that? I don't think I'm exactly anything to be proud of."

Tucker took his other hand and looked him directly in the eye. "You're wrong. I think he would be happy. He is so alone in the world. You're a good man, Chad, whether you realize it or not, and I know that Jamie would be very happy to feel connected to you. He would be very proud to discover that he is your brother."

Chad looked at her wordlessly for a moment, as if he were deciding whether to believe her, then kissed her gently. "Thank you. Maybe you're right. Maybe I will tell him."

"Promise?"

He hesitated, but only for a moment. "I promise I'll think about it."

Jamie caught sight of them and waved wildly. "Hey, Chad! Tucker! Come take a look at this!" He was bent over a tide pool exposed by low tide.

Chad and Tucker carefully picked their way over the slippery rocks to where Jamie was staring into the shallow water. The small basin of captured water was a microcosm of sea life: tiny fish darted among wispy grasses, a purple sea urchin clung to its rock, and an anemone waved its arms seductively.

"This is so cool! Look at all this stuff. Just like an aquarium, but better!" Jamie's eyes shone with the pleasure of discovery.

"You're right about that." Chad hunkered down on one knee, next to Jamie. "An aquarium is great, but it's just an imitation of nature. The real thing is always better." Chad took one of Jamie's crackers and ground it up very fine. He sprinkled a few crumbs into the water, and the tiny fish came to the surface to feed on the specks of white.

"How long will they all be stuck in here?" Jamie trailed his fingers over the surface of the tide pool, and the fish darted for cover in the rocky crevices. "If I were a fish, I would want to be able to swim wherever I wanted." Jamie's voice was suddenly pensive, and Tucker wondered if he were thinking of all the moves he'd been through, like he was just a piece of furniture to be shipped and stored at someone else's whim.

"Don't worry. When the tide comes back up in a couple of hours, they'll be free again." Chad stood up and looked out across the harbor to the open ocean. The mainland was shrouded in fog. "I want to show you a few things." He began to pick his way across the rocks back to the boardwalk, then turned back. "Come on, we don't have much time."

Tucker and Jamie joined Chad on the boardwalk. "Where are we going?" Jamie looked ready for anything.

Chad stared out over the harbor, his gaze settling at a point somewhere in the middle of the moorings. Tucker followed his line of sight. What was he thinking?

"I want you to see some more of what's going on underneath the water. Let's go to Lovers' Cove." Chad put his large hand at Jamie's narrow back and gently steered him toward the dinghy dock.

"You mean in a boat?"

"I wasn't planning on swimming."

The three of them barely fit in the dinghy, but it was a short trip out to the *Irene*. Chad tied up to the mooring next to the old boat. "You two stay here for a minute. I'll get everything ready."

Chad hopped up onto the foredeck of the glass bottom boat. He moved about the boat, quickly reviewing its condition. In the full light of morning, things weren't nearly as bad as he had thought when he'd first seen the *Irene*. A little elbow grease, and she might be a decent boat again.

He peeled off the stained canvas from the passenger area, folding the covers loosely and stowing them below the foredeck. The upholstery was clean, and free of holes. It looked as if the old man had kept things up pretty well after all. For some reason, the realization pleased him.

He popped open a panel and reconnected some wires. "Keep your fingers crossed. I hope this old battery has still got some juice." Behind the wheel, he pressed the starter and the engine turned over, coughed twice, then died. "Come on, baby." He tried again, with no success, but the third time the engine started immediately, and Chad felt a sudden burst of pride in the old boat.

Tucker accepted Chad's hand as he helped her aboard, and Jamie followed close behind. The old boat had three large glass viewing windows set into the hull, with high sides like giant metal boxes. A padded bench ran around the inside perimeter, and a solid overhang covered the seating area, shielding the viewing area from the glare of the sun.

"Okay, folks, take your seats. It's time for the deluxe tour." Tucker and Jamie sat on opposite sides of the first viewing window, closest to the front of the boat. Chad released the boat from its mooring and took his place behind the wheel. He eased the *Irene* into gear.

Tucker listened with amazement as Chad dropped back into the friendly patter he had done years ago. "Good morning, folks, and welcome aboard the *Irene*. My name is Chad, and I'll be your captain and guide for the tour today. As you can see, the *Irene* is a glass-bottom boat. What most people don't know is that the very first glass-bottom boat was invented right here on Catalina Island more than one hundred years ago. Now today you will find them all over the world, but it all started right here on our island."

They reached the edge of the harbor and rounded the point into Lovers' Cove. Tucker looked out over the calm surface of the cove, and the small waves that broke gently over the rocky beach. Had the water been this smooth the day that Irene Carver drowned? She studied Chad from behind her dark glasses, wondering what dark memories he was silently reliving. He had dropped his commentary for the moment, and was searching the coastline, from the beach to the small outcropping of rocks that defined the east end of the cove.

Jamie sat with his elbows on the padded edge of the viewing window, watching the world beneath the water come into view. It was obvious he'd never seen anything like it before. Long strands of seaweed formed a forest for garibaldi to dart between, bright flashes of gold appearing and disappearing in the moving shadows.

"What's that fish? The bright yellow one?" Jamie pointed and asked the question without looking up from the glass, afraid to miss anything.

Chad broke from his reverie and was instantly back in character, the friendly guide. "That, young man, is the state fish of California. The blue ones are garibaldi, too, but they're the young ones. They're blue when they're born, and they change colors later."

"They change colors? Cool. How do they do that?"

Chad put the engine in neutral and joined them at the window. "We don't know exactly how; they just do it." He pointed to the long, thick strands of seaweed. "See the bulbs on that kelp?"

"Yeah. Looks like little balloons."

"Exactly. Except they're not filled with air. They're filled with a kind of methane gas. If you get enough of them, you can actually power a car with the stuff."

"You're kidding."

"No, I'm not. Nature invented almost everything way before humans did."

"Wow. Cool." Jamie studied the seaweed with newfound respect.

Chad sat down next to Jamie and stared into the clear water. Tucker could read the line of tension that spread across the width of Chad's shoulders and the column of his neck, but when he spoke his voice was even.

"Jamie, I talked to Mrs. Hansen on the phone this morning," he said without taking his eyes from the glass below. Tucker thought she saw Jamie stiffen at the mention of the case worker's name.

"Yeah?" A trace of Jamie's hard attitude crept back into his voice. "She's gross. She smells like mothballs." Jamie stared straight down, not looking at Chad. He kicked one foot aimlessly against the base of the window.

"She said you have to go back to the mainland today. I'm sorry, I really wanted you to stay with me and Tucker for a couple of days. I had hoped we could do some more things together, get to know the island a little."

"Oh. No big deal." Jamie had his cool, detached mask back in place, but it was not as convincing as when he had arrived on the island. Tucker guessed that he didn't want to let them know that he was scared to go back. She wondered if he already knew about Lemonwood.

Jamie stood up straight. "So when do I have to go?"

Chad cleared his throat, and Tucker felt the emotion that was unexpressed in his words. "Your plane leaves in a couple of hours. I'm sorry, Jamie. There wasn't anything I could do."

Jamie shrugged, and stared out toward the open

ocean. "That's okay." His eyes were cool and guarded. "I guess there wasn't any point in hanging around here anyway."

Tucker and Chad exchanged looks over the boy's head. Tucker read the anguish in Chad's eyes. She wanted to touch him, to offer some comfort, some reassurance, but she didn't know what to do or say.

They all stared down into the water below for several long minutes without speaking. Eventually, Chad returned to the wheel and put the boat back into gear. A few minutes later, they reached the mooring and Chad secured the boat again. Jamie and Tucker helped him unfold the canvas covers over the passenger area and tie them down.

All three of them were silent for the length of the drive to the airport. Chad drove, and when they reached the airport he parked as far away from the terminal as possible. Jamie hopped out of the cab and took a few steps away, off from the parking area to a small group of rocks.

He climbed up on the highest one and turned slowly around, as if taking in the enormity of the ocean that surrounded the island. Tucker felt the boy's unspoken thought that he would probably never see this again. Her throat ached with unshed tears for all the moving, all the goodbyes Jamie had faced in his life.

Chad and Tucker walked over to join Jamie.

From the boy's vantage point on the rock, he was taller than both of them.

"What do you see?" asked Tucker.

"Water. Just a lot of water." Jamie looked down at Chad. "Thanks for showing me around. It was fun." He scrambled down to a lower boulder that put him on Chad's eye level. "Can I ask you something?"

Chad smiled, a quiet, sad expression. "Sure. Ask me anything."

Jamie looked down at his feet momentarily, as if gathering courage, then directly into Chad's eyes. Tucker noticed that their eyes were the same color, a deep shade that moved between blue and green.

"Can we stay friends? We could write to each other, and maybe I could come back and visit you here someday."

"Of course, we'll stay friends." Chad put his hand on Jamie's shoulder and looked into the eyes that now met him head on. Tucker thought she saw a flicker of decision pass over him, but it was so quick she couldn't be sure.

"Jamie, I've got to tell you something." Chad's voice was gentle in a way that Tucker hadn't heard. "I haven't told you something very important, and I don't want you to leave without hearing it from me."

Jamie waited, silent, never taking his eyes from Chad's face. "We're going to stay friends, always. We're already more than friends, Jamie. We're brothers.''

Jamie's face betrayed that, although he didn't fully understand what Chad was saying, on some gut-level basis, he recognized it as the truth. He didn't speak for a long moment, while he looked at Chad appraisingly, as if really seeing him for the first time.

"Brothers? For real?" His voice was filled with a hope that was afraid of expression.

"Yes. For real. Joshua was my father, too. He was married to my mother many years ago, a long, long time before he met your mom." Chad's voice cracked slightly, and he cleared his throat. "So you're not going to get rid of me, Jamie, even if you want to. We're connected. The two of us are going to have a lot of good times, you'll see. You can come back to Catalina soon, I promise you.''

Chad picked Jamie up and lifted him down off the rock. He carefully set him down. Jamie stepped back and looked up at Chad, solemnly studying his face, feature by feature. Finally satisfied with his evaluation, he turned to Tucker. "I guess we do kind of look alike.''

Tucker smiled. "Yes, I guess you do.''

Chad ruffled the boy's hair. "Come on, kid. If we don't hurry, you're going to miss your plane.'' Chad retrieved Jamie's suitcase and backpack from the bed of the truck.

The three were silent for the short walk to the

waiting plane. The asphalt shimmered in the heat of the late summer sun. They stopped at the base of the steps to the plane.

Jamie turned to Tucker. "It was very nice to meet you. I hope I can ride one of those mopeds next time I'm here." He extended his hand to her gravely.

"Maybe. We'll see." She shook the boy's hand. "It was nice to meet you, too, Jamie."

Jamie turned to Chad and started to extend his hand, but Chad swept him up in his arms and hugged him fiercely. Jamie returned the embrace with rough emotion. Chad let him go, but kept his hands on the boy's shoulders. "I'll talk to you soon, okay? I'm not going to forget about you."

"Okay. I won't forget either. I promise." Jamie slipped on his backpack and picked up his sad-looking suitcase. "Goodbye, Chad. Goodbye, Tucker."

He climbed the steps slowly. At the top, he turned back and waved slowly with his free hand. Tucker felt the tears she had held back so carefully overcome her resistance. A moment later, Jamie disappeared inside the plane.

Chad took her in his arms, wordlessly comforting her. He held her for a moment, then led her away from the plane to the waiting area in front of the terminal. The engines caught with a loud roar. They stood together, arms around one another, as the plane slowly taxied to take off position. Tucker and Chad waved as the plane lifted off, and they kept waving as it grew smaller and smaller, until it was only a tiny dot disappearing in the blue.

Tucker felt a crushing sadness in her chest, a growing pressure that was making it hard for her to breathe. She angrily brushed away the tears from her face with her knuckles. There was no point in crying. None of this had anything to do with her anyway. She had better remember that. She had plenty of her own troubles to think about. She had her life, and Chad Carver and Jamie had their own lives. They would each have to do the best that they could.

Tucker slowly pulled away from Chad. He let her slip from his arm, and he continued to stare off into the sky where the plane had disappeared. She started walking quickly back to her truck. She didn't want Chad to see how much she was hurting right now.

"Tucker, wait." Chad sounded surprised, as if he had just realized she was gone. She didn't turn around. She increased her pace until she was nearly running. She was almost there. She reached out for the door handle, and she felt Chad's hand on her shoulder.

"Tucker, please wait." He pulled her into his arms. "What's the matter? Where are you going?" He held her at arm's length, staring into her eyes, searching her face.

"Chad, I'm sorry." She fought to keep her

voice calm. "I can't keep doing this. I can't keep seeing you, sharing things with you, when I know it will all be over soon. I care about you too much."

Chad was looking at her closely, studying her. She forced herself to continue. "I didn't mean for things to happen this way. I think we had both better do what we have to do, so we can get on with our lives."

Chad nodded. "You're right. Both of us need to put the past behind us and move forward. You were the one who made me understand that. I'm grateful to you."

Chad released her arms and turned away, staring off toward the horizon. He shoved his hands into his pockets. "I don't want to be shackled to the past any longer. You convinced me I had to take responsibility for the present. So I've been doing a lot of thinking over the past few days, and I've made some decisions."

Tucker nodded, silent. She waited for him to continue. She desperately wanted for this to be over, to stop the pain of loss that was growing greater within her with each passing moment. She needed to get away.

"Three big decisions, actually. The first is that I'm staying here."

"What? What do you mean?" She couldn't believe what he was saying.

"I'm staying on Catalina. This island is my

home. I'm not a whole person when I'm away. I've been all over the world trying to feel right, but it never worked. No other place ever felt right; not like Catalina. This island's a part of me. I realized that when Jamie was here. I don't want to lose that part of me again."

Tucker felt her heart beating within her, a strange tattoo of fear and desire. She didn't want to dare to hope what Chad remaining on the island might mean. She must not start to hope for something that would never be.

"The second thing I've decided is, I'm going to ask the court for custody of Jamie." Chad's eyes were dark with emotion. "It'll probably be a fight, I know that. I'm not the ideal candidate for raising a ten-year-old boy. I'm certainly not perfect, but I'm the only family he has. And I think I understand what he's been through. I know what it's like to be alone. I want to make it easier for him, if I can. I just need to convince the judge of that."

Tucker struggled to keep her voice even, but her surging emotions were making it impossible. "Chad, I think that's great. It's a big challenge to raise a child. I know you'll be wonderful with him. He really needs you." She felt a surge of fierce pride in this man, this man she loved.

"Well, I'm not planning on doing it all on my own."

"What do you mean?" A strange, fluttery feeling started low in her stomach, and was working its way up to her chest, to her strongly beating heart.

Chad cleared his throat several times, but when he spoke his voice was still ragged. "I was hoping you might consider getting married."

"What?" She needed to hear it again, needed to hear him say the words.

"To me, I mean. I love you, Tucker P. Ryan. And I don't want to lose you, either." He gently drew her close to him, his eyes locked into hers. "Will you marry me?"

Tucker drew him close to her, and in that moment she was flooded with an overwhelming sensation of tranquility and rightness, a sensation so strong it drove out all fear and uncertainty. She looked into his eyes—eyes the color of the sea.

"Yes, Chad, I will. I think I will marry you."

_____ EPILOGUE _____

The long, low whistle sounded its warning blast. Tucker quickly finished counting the racks of bikes and checked the total against her clipboard. She sighed in exasperation. In ten minutes the last boat would leave the island, and she was still short four units.

"Jamie!"

"Yes?"

The boy appeared from inside the shop, screwdriver in hand. He must have grown six inches in the last twelve months, she thought. His deep tan made his eyes a startling shade of blue. A breeze ruffled his fine blond hair. He pushed it out of his eyes.

"The boat's leaving, and we've still got four bikes out."

"Oh, great. Should I go look for them?"

"Yes, I think you'd better." Tucker checked her clipboard. "It must be that family from Pennsylvania. Take a look and see if they're on their way."

Jamie trotted out the gate. He shaded his eyes with his hand and peered back toward Island Plaza. He yelled back to Tucker. "I see them. They're still way down the street in the middle of town, walking their bikes. It looks like they've stopped for ice cream."

"Run down there quick and tell them if they don't hurry they'll be swimming back to the mainland." Jamie dashed down the street.

Tucker looked out over the yard. Everything else was in place. This had been the busiest Labor Day weekend she could ever remember. For most of the weekend, she'd had every one of her bikes out on rental. She was grateful for the business, but she would be glad when it was all over.

Less than two minutes later, Jamie was back, riding one of the missing bicycles. He hopped off and quickly racked it. Chad appeared right behind him on another bike. He skidded to a stop, spraying gravel everywhere.

"Come on, Chad, no showing off. We've got one more trip!" Jamie disappeared out the gate.

"Don't worry, I'm right behind you." Chad

racked the bike and paused long enough to give
Tucker a quick kiss. "I ran into Jamie by the pier.
He enlisted my help."

"How was your day?" Tucker wrapped her
arms around him.

"Great. Six full trips, and not one passenger
with motion sickness. The *Irene* is a fine boat."

Tucker kissed him full on the mouth. "The captain is pretty okay, too."

"Now that's the way to greet the sailor home
from the sea." He kissed her again, and she felt
her body's familiar response to him. Chad pulled
away with reluctance. "I'll be right back. If I'm
not careful, Jamie will have me fired." He trotted
out the gate and back down the street in the direction Jamie had gone.

A few minutes later, Chad and Jamie were back
with the remaining two bikes. "Jamie sent them
on to the boat. They should be able to make it in
time." They put the last two bikes in their places.

Tucker came out from the shop. "It's over!"
She did a spontaneous little dance of joy, and
embraced Jamie and Chad together, encircling
both of them in her loving arms. "I can't believe
another summer is already over. Now we can
finally relax a little."

"It was a great summer, Tucker." Chad's eyes
glowed with layers of meaning.

"The best ever, I think. In fact, I believe—"

Tucker was interrupted by a familiar, insistent crying coming from the back of the shop.

"Uh oh, sounds like somebody's hungry again." Jamie wiggled out of their three-way embrace. "I'll get her." He ran into the shop.

The two took this opportunity for a slow, luxurious kiss. "Thanks for everything." Chad kissed her again. "And I do mean everything."

"Thank you." Tucker ran her hands through Chad's hair and held his face close to hers. "For everything."

Jamie walked slowly out of the shop, a tiny bundle squirming in his arms. Tucker took her baby girl from him, and she settled down in the familiar comfort of her mother's arms.

The long, low whistle of the big boat sounded again. "Let's go watch the last boat of the summer!" Jamie rounded them all up and they strolled together out to the street, Chad's arm around Tucker and the baby, and Jamie running ahead.

The big boat was slowly pulling away from the dock to begin its passage back to the mainland. The late afternoon sunlight glittered on the surface of the harbor, and a light breeze fluttered the halyards of the moored boats against their masts.

Tucker looked first at her baby, then at the little boy now throwing rocks into the harbor, and then finally at the man she loved. Chad met her eyes, read the love in them, and drew her closer to him.

She nestled into the warm, protective crook of his arm.

The sun was moving lower in the sky, bathing the island, her beloved Catalina, in the fading glow of the late summer day. A sea bird called overhead, spreading an expanse of white wings against the blue sky.

Tucker was in the place she loved most of all, surrounded by the people she loved more than anything.

She was finally home.

SHARE THE FUN . . .
SHARE YOUR NEW-FOUND TREASURE!!

You don't want to let your new books out of your sight?
That's okay. Your friends can get their own. Order below.

No. 25 LOVE WITH INTEREST by Darcy Rice
Stephanie & Elliot find $47,000,000 *plus* interest—true love!

No. 26 NEVER A BRIDE by Leanne Banks
The last thing Cassie wanted was a relationship. Joshua had other ideas.

No. 27 GOLDILOCKS by Judy Christenberry
David and Susan join forces and get tangled in their own web.

No. 28 SEASON OF THE HEART by Ann Hammond
Can Lane and Maggie's newfound feelings stand the test of time?

No. 29 FOSTER LOVE by Janis Reams Hudson
Morgan comes home to claim his children but Sarah claims his heart.

No. 30 REMEMBER THE NIGHT by Sally Falcon
Joanna throws caution to the wind. Is Nathan fantasy or reality?

No. 31 WINGS OF LOVE by Linda Windsor
Mac & Kelly soar to new heights of ecstasy. Are they ready?

No. 32 SWEET LAND OF LIBERTY by Ellen Kelly
Brock has a secret and Liberty's freedom could be in serious jeopardy!

No. 33 A TOUCH OF LOVE by Patricia Hagan
Kelly seeks peace and quiet and finds paradise in Mike's arms.

No. 34 NO EASY TASK by Chloe Summers
Hunter is wary when Doone delivers a package that will change his life.

No. 35 DIAMOND ON ICE by Lacey Dancer
Diana could melt even the coldest of hearts. Jason hasn't a chance.

No. 36 DADDY'S GIRL by Janice Kaiser
Slade wants more than Andrea is willing to give. Who wins?

No. 37 ROSES by Caitlin Randall
It's an inside job & K.C. helps Brett find more than the thief!

No. 38 HEARTS COLLIDE by Ann Patrick
Matthew finds big trouble and it's spelled P-a-u-l-a.

No. 39 QUINN'S INHERITANCE by Judi Lind
Gabe and Quinn share an inheritance and find an even greater fortune.

No. 40 CATCH A RISING STAR by Laura Phillips
Justin is seeking fame; Beth helps him find something more important.

No. 41 SPIDER'S WEB by Allie Jordan
Silvia's quiet life explodes when Fletcher shows up on her doorstep.

No. 42 TRUE COLORS by Dixie DuBois
Julian helps Nikki find herself again but will she have room for him?

No. 43 DUET by Patricia Collinge
Adam & Marina fit together like two perfect parts of a puzzle!

No. 44 DEADLY COINCIDENCE by Denise Richards
J.D.'s instincts tell him he's not wrong; Laurie's heart says trust him.

No. 45 PERSONAL BEST by Margaret Watson
Nick is a cynic; Tess, an optimist. Where does love fit in?

No. 46 ONE ON ONE by JoAnn Barbour
Vincent's no saint but Loie's attracted to the devil in him anyway.

No. 47 STERLING'S REASONS by Joey Light
Joe is running from his conscience; Sterling helps him find peace.

No. 48 SNOW SOUNDS by Heather Williams
In the quiet of the mountain, Tanner and Melaine find each other again.
